WAITING FOR THE GHOST

Sam and the Wakefield twins had been standing in the cemetery for half an hour.

"Tell me about the ghost," Jessica said. "What did he do? Did you see him float out of his grave and fly in the air? What did he look like?"

"He looked like me," Sam said.

"But ghosts don't look like people," Jessica said.

Sam frowned and turned away. Part of him wanted Elizabeth and Jessica to be around if the ghost came. But part of him wanted to be alone. After all, something had been making *him* come to the cemetery, not them.

Suddenly a scream pierced the air. Sam spun around and saw Jessica clutching Elizabeth's arm. Jessica was pointing toward the cemetery gate. Sam followed her gaze. Only fifty yards away the ghost stood frozen. Sam was staring right into its eyes. The ghost's hair, his face, his expression, everything about him looked exactly like Sam.

"He's going to

Natalie Gaurlap

The SWEET VALLEY TWINS series, published by Bantam Books. Ask your bookseller for any titles you have missed

good

1. BEST FRIENDS ✓   good ✓
2. TEACHER'S PET ✓   good
3. THE HAUNTED HOUSE ✓   good
4. CHOOSING SIDES   good
5. SNEAKING OUT ✓   good
6. THE NEW GIRL   good
7. THREE'S A CROWD ✓   good
8. FIRST PLACE ✓
9. AGAINST THE RULES ✓
10. ONE OF THE GANG ✓
11. BURIED TREASURE ✓
12. KEEPING SECRETS ✓
13. STRETCHING THE TRUTH
14. TUG OF WAR ✓
17. BOYS AGAINST GIRLS ✓
18. CENTRE OF ATTENTION ✓
19. THE BULLY ✓
20. PLAYING HOOKY ✓
21. LEFT BEHIND
22. OUT OF PLACE
32. JESSICA ON STAGE ✓
33. ELIZABETH'S NEW HERO

37. THE WAR BETWEEN THE TWINS ✓
38. LOIS STRIKES BACK ✓
39. JESSICA AND THE MONEY
    MIX-UP ✓
40. DANNY MEANS TROUBLE
41. THE TWINS GET CAUGHT ✓
42. JESSICA'S SECRET ✓
43. ELIZABETH'S FIRST KISS
44. AMY MOVES IN
45. LUCY TAKES THE REINS
46. MADEMOISELLE JESSICA
47. JESSICA'S NEW LOOK
48. MANDY MILLER FIGHTS BACK ✓
49. THE TWINS' LITTLE SISTER
50. JESSICA AND THE SECRET STAR
51. ELIZABETH THE IMPOSSIBLE
52. BOOSTER BOYCOTT ✓
53. THE SLIME THAT ATE SWEET
    VALLEY ✓
54. THE BIG PARTY WEEKEND ✓
55. BROOKE AND HER ROCK-STAR
    MUM ✓

SWEET VALLEY TWINS SUPER CHILLERS

1. THE CHRISTMAS GHOST ✓
2. THE GHOST IN THE GRAVEYARD ✓
3. THE CARNIVAL GHOST ✓

SWEET VALLEY TWINS SUPER EDITIONS

1. THE CLASS TRIP ✓
4. THE UNICORNS GO HAWAIIAN ✓

SWEET VALLEY TWINS
◇ SUPER CHILLER ◇

The Ghost in the Graveyard

◇

Written by
Jamie Suzanne

Created by
FRANCINE PASCAL

BANTAM BOOKS
NEW YORK · TORONTO · LONDON · SYDNEY · AUCKLAND

THE GHOST IN THE GRAVEYARD
A BANTAM BOOK 0 553 40132 7

Originally published in U.S.A. by Bantam Skylark Books

First publication in Great Britain

PRINTING HISTORY
Bantam edition published 1991
Bantam edition reprinted 1991, 1992
Sweet Valley High ® and Sweet Valley Twins are registered
trademarks of Francine Pascal

Conceived by Francine Pascal.

Produced by Daniel Weiss Associates, Inc., 33 West 17th Street,
New York, NY 10011

Cover art by James Mathewuse.

Bantam Books are published by Transworld Publishers
Ltd., 61–63 Uxbridge Road, Ealing, London W5 5SA, in
Australia by Transworld Publishers (Australia) Pty. Ltd.,
15–23 Helles Avenue, Moorebank, NSW 2170, and in New
Zealand by Transworld Publishers (N.Z.) Ltd., 3 William
Pickering Drive, Albany, Auckland.

Printed and bound in Great Britain by
Cox & Wyman Ltd., Reading

One

◇

"How can you read in the lunchroom, Elizabeth?"

Elizabeth Wakefield turned a page as her twin sister, Jessica, slid into the seat next to her. The lunchroom at Sweet Valley Middle School was filling up quickly. It was the last day of school before spring vacation, and the lunchroom was even noiser than usual.

"Easy. This is a ghost story, and I'm just getting to the best part," Elizabeth explained.

Jessica made a face. "But it's almost spring vacation," she wailed. "Aren't you even excited?"

"Sure I am," Elizabeth said, still trying to concentrate on her book. Then she looked up and laughed at the expression on Jessica's face. Jessica could never understand why Elizabeth thought books were so interesting.

The Wakefield twins both had long, sun-streaked blond hair, blue-green eyes the color of the Pacific Ocean, and dimples in their left cheeks that showed when they smiled. But even though the twins looked exactly alike, their personalities were completely different.

Jessica was spontaneous, and was always trying something new. She was a member of the exclusive Unicorn Club, which only the prettiest and most popular girls at Sweet Valley Middle School were asked to join. Together, the Unicorns shopped, gossiped, and talked about the cutest boys in the school, and Jessica particularly liked to dominate their conversations. As far as she was concerned, no party really got started until she arrived. That didn't leave much time in her schedule for serious things, like schoolwork.

Elizabeth loved to read and hoped to be a writer someday. She was editor of *The Sweet Valley Sixers*, the sixth-grade newspaper she had founded. She was by far the more serious twin and couldn't understand why Jessica liked to spend so much time with the Unicorns. Elizabeth thought they were all snobs, not at all like her own group of friends. At the same time, Jessica thought that most of her sister's friends were boring.

Despite their differences, Elizabeth and Jessica shared a bond that nobody else could understand. Sometimes they didn't even need to talk to communicate. It was as if they could read each other's minds.

"Well, what's the story about?" Jessica asked, looking over Elizabeth's shoulder. "Is it really scary?"

Elizabeth nodded. "There's this girl," she began in a spooky voice. "And she thinks somebody is following her, but whenever she looks, she never sees anyone there."

"It sounds creepy," Jessica said with a shiver. "What happens?"

"One day," Elizabeth continued, her eyes twinkling, "she goes into the lunchroom at school, sits in her regular seat, and then . . . the monster catches her!" she yelled, grabbing her sister's arm.

"Aaaah!" Jessica screamed. Elizabeth couldn't help laughing. Jessica frowned at her twin. "Ha ha, Liz," she said, trying to look mad, and then collapsed into giggles.

"Sorry," Elizabeth said. "I couldn't resist."

Caroline Pearce came over to their table and sat down. "What's so funny?" she asked.

"It was just a silly joke," Elizabeth said, still smiling.

Jessica didn't say anything. Caroline was the biggest gossip in Sweet Valley Middle School. She had lived on Jessica and Elizabeth's street since they were all in kindergarten, and she was always trying to find out their secrets—and everyone else's.

"You want to know what I heard?" Caroline said in a whisper.

"What?" Jessica asked in a suspicious tone.

"I heard—" Caroline stopped and looked over her left shoulder, then over her right shoulder. She leaned closer to the twins. "I heard a new family is moving in down the street from us tomorrow."

"Oh, everyone knows that already," Jessica said, sounding bored. She took a bite of her sandwich.

"Yeah, but did you know that they have a boy our age?" Caroline asked. She looked pleased with herself.

Jessica raised her eyebrows. "A sixth grader?" she asked.

Caroline nodded. "And he's really cute, too. At least that's what I heard."

"I wonder if he's going on the boat trip on Sunday," Jessica said. The entire sixth grade class was taking a day-long boat ride during spring vacation. Everyone had been talking about it for weeks.

Caroline shrugged. "Who knows? But maybe we can find out tonight."

"I thought you said they were moving in tomorrow," Elizabeth said.

"The *moving* van is coming tomorrow," Caroline said. "My parents said the people might come tonight."

Jessica sat back and frowned. Elizabeth could tell her twin was thinking hard. She had a feeling the Unicorns were going to have a lot to talk about once Jessica had met the new boy.

"Why don't we go over and invite him, then?" Elizabeth suggested. "If he doesn't come on the boat trip with us he won't be able to meet anybody from school for two weeks."

The bell rang, signaling the end of lunchtime, and Caroline stood up. "See you guys later," she said over her shoulder as she joined the group crowding out of the lunchroom.

But Jessica didn't move. She was biting her bottom lip as if she were carefully considering Elizabeth's idea. "Let's not invite him until we can find out a little about him," she said slowly.

Elizabeth gave her sister a startled look. "You mean, you want to wait until you see whether he's cute enough to invite?"

"That's *not* what I meant," Jessica said, blushing. "Come on. Tell me the rest of the ghost story on the way to class."

Elizabeth sighed. It was just like Jessica to change the subject when the situation got uncomfortable.

*   *   *

"You're going to *read?*" the twins' older brother Steven asked. He shook his head. "I must be hallucinating." It was after dinner that same night. Jessica had just announced that she was going into the living room to read.

Jessica lifted her chin. "What's so amazing about that?" she demanded.

Elizabeth giggled. She knew that the only reason Jessica was going to "read" was so she could spend some time in the living room, which had a big window that faced the street. From that strategic viewpoint Jessica could see what was going on outside.

A few minutes after Jessica left the kitchen, Elizabeth followed her into the living room. "What are you going to read?" she asked her twin as she sank down next to her on the couch. *"The Arrival of the New Boy?"*

Jessica tried to look puzzled. "I've never heard of that book," she said innocently. She picked up the latest issue of *Teen Idol* and flipped it open.

Elizabeth just smiled and opened her ghost story.

"What was that noise?" Jessica said, jumping up. She pushed the curtains farther open and looked out the window.

"See anything?" Elizabeth asked.

"Nope." Jessica sat down and looked at her magazine. After a few minutes, she stood up again. "I think I'll get a glass of milk," she said.

On her way to the kitchen, Jessica stood by the window and looked up and down the street. She let out a sigh of disappointment.

"Nothing yet?" Elizabeth asked.

Jessica put her hands on her hips and frowned at her sister. "Why do you keep asking that, Lizzie? I'm not looking for anything."

"Oh, right," Elizabeth said, nodding. "I just had this crazy idea that you might be watching for the new family and the cute boy."

"Me? Who do you think I am, Caroline Pearce?" Jessica said, pretending to be shocked.

Elizabeth giggled.

For the next two hours, Jessica kept springing up off the couch and finding reasons to look out the window. But each time she looked there was nobody there. Eventually it became too dark to see anyone, even if they did arrive. And that meant there was no chance of seeing the new boy until the next day.

"I'm going upstairs," Jessica muttered in a disappointed tone. She threw her magazine on the table and stalked out of the room.

Elizabeth smiled to herself. Finally she could read her ghost story in peace.

Two

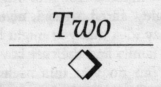

"You're *still* sleeping?" Jessica exclaimed as she burst into Elizabeth's room the next morning.

"What's wrong?" Elizabeth asked, sitting up in bed.

"Wrong?" Jessica asked. "Nothing. Why?"

Elizabeth flopped back onto the bed. "Something must be wrong or you wouldn't be up so early."

"I just thought you might like to meet the new boy," Jessica explained as she opened Elizabeth's curtains with a jerk.

Elizabeth turned to look at her clock, which said 8:07. "Jess, this is the first day of spring vacation. I can't believe you're doing this."

"I told you!" Jessica repeated impatiently. "Caroline Pearce just called to tell me that the new boy is super cute and he's moving in this very minute. We have to go meet him."

"You go meet him, Jess," Elizabeth said with a yawn. "I'm going back to sleep."

"No you're not," Jessica said, pulling Elizabeth's covers off. "Get up right now!"

Elizabeth giggled. That was what *she* always said when she wanted to get Jessica out of bed for school.

"OK," Elizabeth said, reluctantly rolling out of bed. She knew it was useless to argue with Jessica when she had her mind set on something.

Before Elizabeth could say anything else, Jessica dashed into her own room through the bathroom connecting the two bedrooms. "What do you think I should wear?" Jessica called to Elizabeth.

"I don't know, Jess," Elizabeth called back.

Taking her time, Elizabeth got dressed in her favorite old blue jeans and a striped T-shirt. She washed her face and pulled her hair into a ponytail. Then she sat down on her bed and picked up the book that was lying on her night table. She knew that she would have to wait while Jessica picked out the perfect outfit, put on some light makeup, and brushed her hair.

Elizabeth had finished almost an entire chapter before Jessica bounced into her room and announced that she was ready.

"For someone who couldn't wait to go, you sure took a long time," Elizabeth teased.

"First impressions are the most important," Jessica said primly. "Now, if you're ready—let's go!"

"Can you believe it?" Elizabeth said as soon as she and Jessica stepped out of their front door. "It looks like it's going to rain on the first day of vacation."

"As long as it clears up by tomorrow," Jessica said. "The boat ride is going to be the best!"

The twins walked quickly until they came to a large brick house down the block. A large moving van was backed into the driveway. Furniture was sitting on the front lawn, and men in dark blue overalls were carrying boxes from the truck into the house.

"Walk slower, Lizzie," Jessica whispered. "I don't see him."

Just then, a boy on a shiny green ten-speed bike came zooming down the steel ramp attached to the back of the moving van. He skidded to a stop when he noticed Elizabeth and Jessica standing across the street. He was a little taller than the twins, and he had very curly black hair. His eyes were a deep, warm brown.

"Hi," Elizabeth called.

"Hi," the boy called back.

Elizabeth crossed the street. "Welcome to the neighborhood. You're moving into a great house," she said. "We knew the people who used to live here. I hope you get the room with the round windows."

Jessica smiled at the boy as she followed Elizabeth across the street.

When Elizabeth was almost to his front yard she introduced herself. "I'm Elizabeth Wakefield, and this is my sister, Jessica."

"We live down the block," Jessica added.

"Hi," the boy replied, smiling. "I'm Sam Sloane. And I *am* getting the room with the round windows. It's really cool."

"Where did you move from?" Jessica asked.

"San Francisco," Sam said.

"Really? I've always wanted to go there," Jessica told him.

"It's a great city," Sam replied, sounding a little sad.

"I guess you'll be going to Sweet Valley Middle School, right?" Elizabeth asked, trying to change the subject.

"Yes. I'll be in the sixth grade," Sam said.

"Great! We're in sixth, too," Jessica said.

"It's too bad we had to move here during vacation, though," Sam continued. "Now I'll have to wait two entire weeks to start meeting people."

"No you won't, Sam," Elizabeth replied. "You can come on the sixth-grade boat ride tomorrow!"

A flash of lightning interrupted Sam before he could answer. Sam, Elizabeth, and Jessica looked up. *One, two, three, four, five, six,* Elizabeth counted to herself before the thunder came. When it did, it rumbled through the air for a long time.

"I heard about the boat ride when I registered for school," Sam said after the thunder had stopped.

"I think it would be great if you'd come," Jessica exclaimed. "That is, if it doesn't rain."

"Will you?" Elizabeth asked.

"I don't think so." Sam hesitated. "I won't know anyone." There was another flash of lightning.

"You know *us*," Jessica said. "That's a start, isn't it?"

"Well, OK," Sam agreed as it began to thunder again. "I'll have to ask my parents, but I guess I'll come."

That time, Elizabeth only counted to three between the lightning and the thunder. "The storm is getting closer!" she informed them.

"You could ride to the marina with us tomorrow morning," Jessica offered. "Our parents won't mind. Come by a few minutes before nine." Jessica pointed out the Wakefields' house a few doors down. "That's where we live."

"OK," Sam said. "Thanks!"

"Hey, Sam!" called a man from the front porch.

"Yeah, Dad?"

"Let's help the movers get everything into the house before the rain hits."

"I guess I'll see you tomorrow," Sam told the twins, and sprinted toward his front door.

"What did you think? Isn't he cute?" Jessica asked Elizabeth as they hurried to their house. "He has the most amazing eyes!"

"Yes, I guess he is cute," Elizabeth had to admit. "And he's definitely very nice."

Just then drops of rain began to fall, and the girls had to pick up their pace. Even though it was a very short distance, they were still drenched from head to toe by the time they reached home. But Jessica was so excited about Sam that she didn't seem to notice.

"I can't wait to find out more about Sam tomorrow on the boat ride," she said happily. "Lila and Ellen will be so jealous when we drive up with him. You know, Lizzie, I think this is going to be the best vacation ever!"

It didn't take Sam long to arrange his furniture. The bed went against the wall, and he put his desk by the window. His new room was very small, so there weren't many decisions to make. As soon as Sam finished he hurried back outside, jumped on his bike, and took off.

The earlier rain shower had ended, but every now and then a jagged bolt of lightning crackled or thunder rumbled over Sam's head. Sam didn't care. He wanted to explore Sweet Valley. And even though he had only gotten into town the day before, he knew exactly where he wanted to go.

Sam and his parents had driven briefly through the town when they had arrived the day before. But the sun had been starting to set, and Sam felt sure that it would look different in the daylight. *It will look different*, Sam thought to himself as he pedaled. *It has to*.

Sam had noticed something very strange the day before—he seemed to know exactly where everything in Sweet Valley was and what it looked like *before* he had seen it.

Sam had been born in Sweet Valley, but he hadn't been back since his natural parents had been killed in a car crash more than eleven years before. He was just a baby. The Sloanes had adopted Sam and taken him to San Francisco when he was nine months old. Could a baby possibly remember how a whole town looked?

When Sam got downtown, he felt again that things around him were familiar. He recognized the houses, the shops, and the grocery stores. Stranger yet, Sam felt as if he belonged there, as if he had never been away from Sweet Valley.

A cold breeze was starting to pick up, but Sam kept riding farther and farther away from his new home. He wasn't just riding aimlessly. He was deliberately choosing turns, heading in a particular direction. It was as if one section of town were pulling him like a magnet. The feeling terrified Sam. He wanted to turn around and go home, but something *made* him keep riding.

After several more turns, Sam got an eerie feeling that he had finally reached his destination, miles from his own neighborhood. The street sign said McClarendon Street. Halfway down the block, Sam came to a stop in front of a crumbling mansion. He recognized it immediately. This was it—this was what had been pulling him, calling to him, although he didn't know why. It was a spooky house. It sat in the middle of a large yard filled with dead flowers and overgrown weeds. A high wrought-iron fence surrounded the property, making it look almost like a jail. Many of the windows were broken, some of the frames were rotting, and the dull gray paint was peeling. It was clear that no one lived there.

Why am I here? Sam wondered.

The wind blew a sheet of newspaper into the spokes of Sam's bicycle. He suddenly felt an overwhelming desire to get away. He jumped on his bike and rode as hard and as fast as he could, heading back to the safety of his own house. But all the way he kept thinking, *I know something about that house. I can feel it. If only I knew what it was.*

"Lizzie?" Jessica asked in a sugary voice.

Elizabeth put down her book and looked at her twin. "What?" she asked, punching her pillow. The clock said 9:30 P.M.

"I was wondering . . ." Jessica fiddled with the doorknob. "Tomorrow when we go on the boat trip . . ."

"You want to borrow something, right?" Elizabeth finished for her. "Let me guess—my new blue and white headband, right?"

"Right!" Jessica laughed. "How did you know?"

"ESP," Elizabeth said. She jumped out of bed and went to her dresser. "It's right here somewhere."

"Well, actually, Lizzie," Jessica began, "I already have it."

Elizabeth looked at her twin. "Why were you so sure I'd say yes?"

"ESP, I guess," Jessica said, grinning. "This boat trip is going to be so much fun, isn't it?"

Elizabeth nodded. "I just hope it doesn't rain."

"It won't," Jessica said confidently. "You'll see."

Three

◇

Sam tossed in his bed from side to side. He knew he was dreaming, but he couldn't wake up. Waves were crashing all around him, and lightning kept slicing through the sky. An old man was trying to get to him, but the wind was too strong. For every step forward, the wind pushed the man two steps back. Sam tried to see the old man's face, but it was too dark. Sam knew it was important to talk to him. The old man was getting farther and farther away.

"Wait!" Sam yelled. "I'm over here!"

Sam sat up in bed, his eyes wide open. His heart was pounding. *Where am I?* he thought, looking around the strange room. Suddenly he remembered the new house in Sweet Valley. And then he realized why he had woken up so suddenly. He had been dreaming the dream again—the horrible nightmare about the storm that never ended. Sam's heart sank as he realized that he hadn't been able to leave the dream behind him in San Francisco.

He freed himself from his twisted covers and went to the window to look outside. *Forget about the nightmare*, he told himself firmly. *Today is going to be terrific.* It was the day of the sixth-grade boat ride, and even though it had stormed during the night, the sky was clear and blue. In fact, it looked like it was going to be a perfect day.

Sam dressed quickly and ran downstairs. His parents were sitting at the kitchen table over mugs of coffee. Half-unpacked boxes were stacked on the floor and on the counters.

As Sam ate a bowl of cereal, his parents discussed how to decorate the house. Sam's father was an architect, and both of his parents were excited about working on the new house. They were going to shop for some furniture while Sam was out on the boat.

Sam tried to think of some suggestions for the house, but he couldn't concentrate. The strange feelings that had been bothering him wouldn't go away.

Finally his mother noticed how quiet he was. "Is everything OK, Sam?" she asked. "Do you like your room?"

"Sure, Mom. It's great." Sam pushed his spoon around in his cereal bowl for a moment. His parents were looking at him. "It's just that ever since we got here, I feel like I've seen all of this before," he explained.

Mr. and Mrs. Sloane looked quickly at each other. "What do you mean, Sam?" his father asked.

"I don't really know," Sam said hesitantly. He looked up. "But there's this house, this old, run-down house. I could swear I've seen it before. Do you think it's possible that I remember it from when I was a baby?" He was hoping they would have a commonsense explanation.

"Well, honey," his mother said gently, "you were only nine months old when we adopted you, and then we moved to San Francisco. I don't *think* you'd remember much."

"Then you don't know anything about an old house on McClarendon Street?" he asked. He felt stupid for asking, but he had to know.

Mr. Sloane shook his head. "We've told you all we know, Sam. I'm sorry."

Sam looked from his mother to his father and back again. They both looked worried. "Forget it," he said, trying to sound cheerful. "It's just a silly feeling I had."

"I hope you're not upset about moving back here," his mother broke in.

"No, it's OK, Mom. Really." Sam pushed

his chair back. He wanted to forget all about the old house and the strange feelings he had been experiencing. "I'd better leave now if I want a ride to the marina for the boat trip. See you later."

His father patted him on the back. "OK, Sam. Have a good time."

Sam climbed into the Wakefields' maroon van with Elizabeth, Jessica, and their father.

"Sit next to the window," Elizabeth told Sam. "That way you'll have a good view of Sweet Valley on the way."

As they rode, the twins pointed out things of interest to Sam.

None of this looks familiar, Sam thought happily. He felt like laughing out loud. But when Mr. Wakefield stopped at an intersection and then turned left, Sam's heart skipped a beat.

"Isn't the marina beautiful, Sam?" Elizabeth asked.

Sam sat perfectly still, as if frozen. *The boats, the docks, the pier, the restaurants*, Sam thought. *It's all so familiar.* He felt as if he'd spent hundreds of afternoons at that very marina.

Something very strange was going on. Sam was sure of it. Somehow he was connected to Sweet Valley. He told himself there had to be a reason he knew so much about the town. But the more he thought about it, the more he feared that there was no reasonable explanation.

"Sam, are you all right?" Elizabeth asked.

Sam didn't answer. He felt weak, and he was afraid that if he said something the Wakefields would hear the panic in his voice.

"I'm fine," Sam croaked out.

The marina was crowded with Sweet Valley Middle School sixth graders.

"Stop here, Dad!" Jessica called out. "There's Lila!"

Mr. Wakefield stopped the car and Jessica immediately jumped out. "I'm going to catch up with Lila," Jessica shouted back to Elizabeth and Sam as she hurried off. "I'll see you on the boat."

Elizabeth was still watching Sam closely. "Are you *sure* nothing's wrong?" she asked again after Mr. Wakefield had driven off.

Looking at Elizabeth, Sam felt he could trust her. She wouldn't make fun of what was happening to him.

"Uh, well," Sam said slowly, "I get this weird feeling. It's like I've been here before." Sam frowned, waiting for Elizabeth's reaction.

"I know what you mean!" Elizabeth said. "It's like you dream something, and then all of a sudden you're living it. It's called déjà vu."

"Well, sort of," Sam said, relieved that Elizabeth hadn't laughed. "But how many times have you felt that way?"

"Oh, I don't know. Maybe once or twice."

"I've been having that feeling since we arrived in Sweet Valley," Sam replied. "And here at the marina it's even worse. Everything is completely familiar. I'm just weird, I guess."

"I don't think you're weird," Elizabeth said. "Maybe it just means you already feel like you belong here." She gave Sam a big smile. "Don't worry about it."

Sam looked at Elizabeth and then at the crowd of kids who were moving toward the end of the pier to meet the boat. *Elizabeth's right*, he told himself. *There's nothing to worry about.*

"Come on, let's go!" Elizabeth said.

As they walked along the dock toward the boat, Elizabeth and Sam passed an old fisherman mending a net. His battered captain's hat was pulled down low over his eyes. He pushed the hat back off his face when he saw Sam.

"Hello there, young man," he said slowly, nodding as he spoke.

Elizabeth nudged Sam. "I think he's talking to you," she said.

"No, he's not," Sam answered. "I don't know him."

"You're taller by a head every time I see you," the fisherman said.

Every time? Sam thought. *What's he talking about?* He caught Elizabeth's arm and practically dragged her down the pier.

"Say hello to your father for me," the man called after them.

"Who was th—?" Elizabeth started to ask, but Sam cut her off.

"I don't know! I've never seen him before in my life!" Sam exclaimed. He let go of Elizabeth's arm. His hands were shaking. "See what I mean?"

"He probably just thought you were someone else," Elizabeth said calmly. "There's nothing to worry about."

Sam couldn't have disagreed more, but he didn't know what to say. He just shrugged. Things were getting weirder by the minute.

By the time Sam and Elizabeth reached the end of the pier, the boat had already docked. All of the sixth graders were pushing to get on board. A girl with shoulder-length light brown hair stood at the top of the gangplank. She was the first one in line.

"That's Lila Fowler," Elizabeth told Sam. "She's Jessica's best friend."

"That's typical Lila," said a girl's voice from behind Sam. "She always has to be the first to do anything." Sam turned around and saw a girl with pale blue eyes and thin blond hair. "Who are you?" the girl asked.

Elizabeth smiled. "Amy, this is Sam Sloane. He just moved in down the block from us. Sam, this is my friend, Amy Sutton."

"Hi," Amy said as they made their way onto the boat. "How do you like Sweet Valley so far?"

Sam shrugged. "It's got some interesting houses," he said with a small laugh.

After Sam, Elizabeth, and Amy got onto the boat, several more girls came up to talk to them. Sam began to wonder whether there were any boys in Sweet Valley. He decided that if there were, he wasn't going to meet them by hanging around the girls.

He excused himself from the girls and walked toward the back of the boat. Some boys were there, but none of them paid attention to Sam, so he walked to a bench by the railing and sat down alone. When the ship set sail and pulled away from the marina, Sam watched the water and listened to the other kids laughing.

"Hey, you can't sit there," Lila said, coming up to Sam a few minutes later. "That's where the Unicorns are going to sit." She was with a group of girls.

Her voice wasn't unfriendly, but it wasn't friendly, either. She seemed to expect Sam to move just because she told him to.

"There's no such thing as a unicorn," he said.

"There is at Sweet Valley Middle School," Lila said firmly. "And this is where we're going to sit."

Suddenly Jessica stepped forward. "Hi, Sam! The Unicorns is the name of our club. This bench is the only place where all of us can sit together.

Would you mind sitting somewhere else?'' She flashed a dazzling smile at him.

Sam thought Jessica was a lot nicer than her best friend. But he noticed that she was being very careful about how she talked around Lila.

''Do you know this guy?'' Lila asked Jessica.

''Sure, Lila. This is Sam Sloane,'' Jessica said. ''He just moved here.''

''Well, he can move again—out of our seats!'' Lila said.

The girls giggled at Lila's joke. Even Jessica laughed.

''No problem,'' Sam said. ''I'm leaving.'' He wandered down to the other end of the boat, where another group of boys stood talking. Sam watched them tell jokes and laugh about things that had happened at school. Nobody said hello or even looked his way.

Finally it was time for lunch—a picnic-style box lunch of chicken, fruit salad, and brownies. Sam took his lunch and ate alone.

Elizabeth walked up to join Sam when he was almost finished eating. ''How's it going?'' she asked.

''OK,'' Sam replied. The truth was, he couldn't wait to get home.

''Jessica and I are having a pool party the day after tomorrow,'' Elizabeth said. ''Would you like to come?''

What for? Sam thought. *So I can feel left out again?* But he shrugged and said, "Sure. Why not?"

"So, who is he?" Lila asked, licking her fingers one at a time.

Jessica crumpled up her paper napkin. "His name is Sam Sloane, I told you. He's new."

"He's cute but he sure acts like a dud," Lila said with a giggle. She was looking down at the other end of the boat.

Some of the other Unicorns laughed along with her. "He doesn't talk to anyone at all," Ellen added.

"Except Elizabeth," Lila remarked. She looked at the others, and gave Jessica a sly smile. "Elizabeth is always so *nice* to everyone."

Jessica lifted her chin. "That's right. She is," she retorted.

"Elizabeth Wakefield, the nicest person in the world," Lila went on in a singsong voice.

Jessica took a long sip of her soda and didn't say anything. Sometimes Lila could be so snobby that it made Jessica want to scream! Just because Elizabeth was nice wasn't any reason for Lila to make fun of her.

Somebody should teach Lila Fowler a lesson, Jessica decided. *Even if she is a Unicorn.*

* * *

"Just wait 'til I get my hands on my sister," Elizabeth muttered to herself as she dashed around the Wakefields' kitchen. The usually tidy room looked like a battle zone. The counters were stacked with dirty dishes and pans, food, and spices.

It was Monday night, the day after the sixth-grade boat ride. But it wasn't just any Monday night, it was the second No-Cooking Monday. The twins had given their mother four No-Cooking Mondays for her birthday. They were supposed to do all the cooking and cleaning up so that Mrs. Wakefield could take it easy. Everyone in the family agreed that it was a wonderful present. Mrs. Wakefield worked part-time as an interior decorator and she was frequently tired in the evenings. The only problem was, Jessica hadn't shown up to help. Again.

The kitchen door flew open and the twins' brother came in. Steven had brown hair and brown eyes, and the twins secretly thought he was beginning to look like a younger version of Mr. Wakefield. They never told Steven they thought so, because they were afraid he'd take it as a compliment. They didn't want Steven's head to get any more swelled than it already was.

"What's up?" Steven asked. He held his backpack in one hand and the last bites of a slice of sausage pizza in the other. "When do we eat? I'm starving."

"Soon," Elizabeth said, checking the clock.

"What are you making, a seven-course dinner?" Steven asked, surveying the messy kitchen.

"It's broiled flounder, Mom's favorite. And don't even try to be funny," Elizabeth said.

"Where's Jessica?" Steven asked. "I thought you two were poisoning us together."

"Ha ha," said Elizabeth.

"Need help tasting anything?" Steven asked, walking toward the stove.

"Stay away from this until dinner, Steven!" Elizabeth warned. She waved a cooking spoon threateningly. "I'll murder you if you even touch anything."

Just then Jessica swept into the kitchen. "Hi, guys," she said. "Hey, something smells great. What's for dinner, Lizzie?"

"Jess, where have you been?" Elizabeth asked. "It's Monday night."

"I know, Lizzie. And I tried really hard to get home early, but my Unicorn meeting took forever."

"And of course you could never walk out on a Unicorn meeting," Steven interrupted, leaning against the refrigerator.

"Steven," Jessica said hotly, "we were discussing something very important at that meeting!"

"Like what?" he asked. "What all of you should wear tomorrow? It would be terrible if any of you wore the same thing by accident," he added, trying to keep a straight face.

Jessica turned her back on her brother. "Listen, Lizzie, I'm sorry. Anyway, you know I'm a terrible cook. I probably wouldn't have been much help."

"You missed last Monday's dinner because the Unicorns were making plans about what to do over vacation. And you weren't here today. You promised we'd do this together, Jess."

"I know, I know. I'll really help out next Monday—I promise. OK?"

"You can help out tonight by doing *all* of the cleanup after we eat," Elizabeth said.

Jessica surveyed the messy kitchen. Panic was written all over her face. Elizabeth and Steven started to laugh.

"Why didn't I think of that?" Jessica said faintly, with a half-smile.

Suddenly Steven slumped to the floor, his back against the refrigerator door. He put the back of his hand to his forehead. "Are we going to eat soon? I'm growing too weak to stand."

"OK, OK," Elizabeth said. "Tell Mom and Dad to come to the table. Jess, help me serve."

Once dinner was on the table, No-Cooking Monday number two was a complete success. The meal was delicious. There were seconds for everyone and, more important, thirds and fourths for Steven.

"Another excellent dinner," Mr. Wakefield said.

"Thanks, Dad," Elizabeth said proudly.

"Thanks, Dad," Jessica echoed.

Elizabeth gave her sister a poisonous look, but Jessica smiled innocently.

"Thank you for the dinner, girls," Mrs. Wakefield said, getting up from the table. "And to think that I don't even have to help clean up!"

"Well," Elizabeth said after her parents had left the room, "come on, Jess, I'll help you clear the table."

Jessica looked at the clock on the wall. "Oh, look at the time!" she cried, jumping to her feet. "It's going to be on any minute."

"What?" Steven asked.

"A movie starring Kent Kellerman is on TV tonight," Jessica said. "It's about a guy who gets reincarnated. I just have to see it! Please, Lizzie, can you clean up tonight? I promise I'll do *everything* next week. Please?" Elizabeth started to protest, but Jessica had already raced into the family room.

Elizabeth stared at the plates on the table and thought about the mess in the kitchen.

"You're going to be washing dishes for hours," Steven observed.

Elizabeth didn't know whether to laugh or cry.

"I'll bet Jessica is reincarnated," she told Steven. "She might have been a human being in a past life—but she's definitely a monster in this one!"

Jessica pounced on the telephone when a commercial came on. She quickly dialed Lila's number.

"Isn't it cool?" she asked without saying hello. "It is *so* spooky."

"Yes. That part where he recognized the lady in the old painting was creepy," Lila agreed. "Do you believe in that stuff?"

Jessica twirled the phone cord around her finger while she thought. "Well, maybe. What if you woke up one day and you suddenly remembered you used to be Jack the Ripper?"

"Be serious," Lila said. "Besides, I'm pretty sure I'm reincarnated."

"Oh, really? What were you?" Jessica giggled. "A person or an animal? I know, you used to be a skunk," she said with a grin.

That gets you back, she told Lila silently. Jessica covered her mouth to hide a laugh. It served Lila right for saying mean things about Elizabeth. She only did it to show off in front of the other Unicorns.

"No," Lila answered in a haughty voice. "For your information, I'm almost positive I was Cleopatra in my past life."

Jessica let out a loud laugh. "Right, Lila. You have so much in common with her."

"I'm *totally* serious," Lila said. "But I don't blame you for laughing. You wouldn't understand."

"What?" Jessica glared at the telephone. "Why wouldn't I under—"

"Oh, the commercials are over," Lila cut in. "See you tomorrow."

Click.

Jessica slammed the receiver down. She let out a growl, then threw a pillow across the room.

"What's with you?" Steven asked, coming into the family room.

"Lila Fowler can act so snobby sometimes. It makes me furious," Jessica grumbled. She slumped down on the couch and crossed her arms.

Steven opened his eyes wide. "But she's a Unicorn," he said in a pretend-shocked voice.

Jessica curled her lip. "Very funny, Steven. I'm really, *really* mad, so you'd better just go away."

"Why don't you get her back if she makes you so mad?" Steven asked.

"I will," Jessica told him, scowling at the television. "As soon as I figure out how."

Four

◇

Elizabeth surveyed the backyard with satisfaction. She had arranged the lawn furniture on the patio, put the latest Johnny Buck cassette on the tape player, and tested the water in the swimming pool. *Well*, Elizabeth thought happily, *it was a lot of work, but I think everything is perfect for the pool party.*

Just then Jessica came out through the sliding glass doors, wearing a silver bathing suit. "Is there anything I can do to help?" she asked.

"Yes. I'm going inside to get into my bathing suit," Elizabeth said. "Do you think you can manage to get the door, if any guests show up?"

"I think I can handle that. But hurry back, Lizzie. I don't want to have to do *all* the work for the party!"

"Jessica!" Elizabeth said in an exasperated voice. "I—"

"I'm kidding!" Jessica interrupted her. "It looks great out here. You did a terrific job."

"Thanks," Elizabeth said with a smile.

When Elizabeth came back outside in a blue tank suit, the party had already started. A large group had arrived and some kids were splashing around in the pool. Lila and Jessica were standing off to the side, talking.

"Peter Burns," Jessica said, giving him a wave. "He's good in science. Who do you think he was?"

"Probably Albert Einstein," Lila decided.

"How about Ginny Lu Culpepper?" Jessica asked. Ginny Lu had been born in Tennessee and had a strong Southern accent. She was great with horses.

"I'll bet she was Annie Oakley or someone from the Wild West," Lila said.

"What are you guys talking about?" Elizabeth asked, joining them.

"Lila and I are deciding who everyone was in a previous life," Jessica explained. "Who do you think you were in a past life, Lizzie?"

Elizabeth thought for a minute. She didn't believe in reincarnation, but it was fun to imagine who she might have been. "I hope I was Florence Nightingale," Elizabeth said with a grin.

"Who's Florence Nightingale?" Jessica asked.

"She was a famous nurse," Elizabeth replied. "She helped a lot of people."

"Figures," Lila mumbled. She looked at Jessica and faked a wide yawn.

"Hi, everyone," Amy Sutton called as she entered the backyard. "Looks like a great party. Why aren't you in the pool, Elizabeth?"

"We're talking about reincarnation," Jessica explained.

"Oh, you must have seen the Kent Kellerman movie last night. Wasn't it great?" Amy asked. "I think everyone watched it."

"Unless they were washing the dinner dishes," Elizabeth said, looking straight at her sister.

"So who do you think you were, Lila?" Amy asked.

"I was Cleopatra, Queen of the Nile," Lila purred.

Amy rolled her eyes at Elizabeth. "Let's go for a swim," she said as she leaned over and grabbed a large beach ball. Amy didn't get along too well with any of the Unicorns. The Unicorns thought she was a tomboy, and she thought they were snobs.

"OK," Elizabeth agreed.

The girls joined a huge game of keep-away that had begun in the pool. When Elizabeth looked up some time later, she noticed Sam sitting by the side of the pool. *Alone again,* she thought to herself.

"I'm going to take a break, you guys," Elizabeth called out. She climbed out of the pool and walked over to where Sam was sitting on a lounge chair.

"Hi, Sam," Elizabeth said. "I'm glad you came. Aren't you coming in the pool?"

Then she noticed the expression on Sam's face. His forehead was wrinkled and he looked like he was deep in thought. "What are you thinking about?" Elizabeth asked.

Sam smiled slowly. "Reincarnation," he said.

"You and everyone else at the party," Elizabeth said. "Do you think you've been reincarnated?" She sat down beside him.

"What would you say if I said yes?" he said.

"Well, that would depend," she said with a little laugh. "Do you think you were George Washington or Elvis Presley?" But when she glanced up at Sam, he wasn't laughing. He was watching her very carefully and seriously.

"What would you *really* do?" Sam asked.

Elizabeth felt a chill crawl up her back as she recalled what Sam had told her at the marina. She tightened her beach towel around her shoulders. Sam sounded so serious. "I think I'd believe you," she said quietly.

"Weird things have been happening ever since I moved to Sweet Valley," Sam continued. "On the marina when I thought everything was familiar and then that man who spoke to me—

well, that still wasn't the strangest thing. The weirdest thing is the house."

"What house?"

"An old mansion on McClarendon Street. I haven't told anyone about it, but I've gone there a couple of times," Sam said.

"Isn't that on the other side of town?" Elizabeth asked.

Sam nodded. "I feel like I *have* to go there, but I don't know why," he said. "Since last night I've been wondering. What if that house was my home in a past life?"

"Hey, Lizzie!" Jessica called from near the house. "People are getting hungry! Come and help me serve the hot dogs."

"I'm coming," Elizabeth shouted back. She looked at Sam. "I've got to help Jess right now. But I want to hear more later. OK?" Sam nodded and Elizabeth headed over to the grill, where Mr. Wakefield was cooking the food.

"Hi, Florence Nightingale," Jessica said, coming up behind Elizabeth with a tray full of hot dogs, hamburgers, buns, mustard, ketchup, and pickles.

Elizabeth didn't answer her.

"Elizabeth?" Jessica said after a moment. "Lizzie, are you listening?"

"Oh!" Elizabeth responded. "I'm sorry, Jess. I didn't hear you."

"You were a million miles away. What's up?" Jessica asked.

"Nothing," Elizabeth said absently.

"Nothing? Come on, Lizzie, you can't fool me. Tell me what's up."

Elizabeth hesitated. Sam hadn't said that what he had told her was a secret. Still, it seemed like too personal a thing to share. But Jessica was staring at Elizabeth, waiting. "Well," Elizabeth said slowly, "I just had a very strange conversation with Sam Sloane."

"What did he say?" Jessica asked.

"Nothing," Elizabeth said.

"Elizabeth, I'm your twin sister," Jessica exclaimed. "You can trust me!"

Elizabeth knew that wasn't always true, but she had to tell someone. She took a deep breath. "Sam thinks he's reincarnated from a former life here in Sweet Valley. I don't think he's kidding. He really, truly believes it," she said.

"I thought you didn't believe in that stuff, Lizzie," Jessica said.

"I don't," Elizabeth replied. "But I think Sam really does."

Suddenly Jessica grabbed Elizabeth's arm. "I just had a super fantastic idea," she hissed. She was looking across the yard at Lila.

"What?" Elizabeth could tell her twin was very excited about something.

"Will you help me play a trick on Lila tonight? She's sleeping over," Jessica went on.

Elizabeth made a face. "What kind of a trick? I don't want to do anything mean."

"It won't be mean, Lizzie, honest." Jessica lowered her voice. "I just want to get back at her for something. Will you help?"

Frowning, Elizabeth looked over at Lila, who was showing off in the middle of a big group of kids. Usually, Elizabeth didn't like to play tricks on people. But if it was just a joke and it wasn't mean, maybe it wouldn't hurt. Lila could take a joke.

"I guess so," Elizabeth decided.

"Great! What you said about Sam was what made me think of it," Jessica said. "Shh—he's coming this way. Oh," she added with a giggle, "here comes Ellen, too. She asked me to introduce her to Sam. She thinks he's cute."

As Jessica introduced Sam to Ellen, other guests crowded around the grill, waiting for hot dogs. Ken Matthews was carrying the beach ball.

"Do you believe in reincarnation?" Ellen asked Sam.

Elizabeth noticed that Sam didn't answer right away. At last he said, "I think I used to be in the circus."

"The circus?" Ellen asked. "Why?"

"I'll show you," Sam said. He pointed to Ken. "Can I have that ball?" Ken bounced it to him. "Jessica, can I have the mustard, please?" Sam asked. Jessica passed the jar to him. "Ellen, how about one of your sneakers?" Ellen reached down and picked up one of her purple running shoes from under a lounge chair.

By this time almost everyone had gathered around Sam. When he started to juggle the ball, mustard, and sneaker, they burst into applause. After juggling for a few minutes, Sam caught everything and took a deep, exaggerated bow.

"Where did you *really* learn to juggle?" Ellen asked Sam when the excitement had died down.

"We had a unit on juggling in my gym class in San Francisco," Sam told them.

"That's cool!" Ken said. For the rest of the party, everyone talked about the differences between going to school in San Francisco and in Sweet Valley.

By the end of the afternoon, Elizabeth knew that the party had been a major success, especially for Sam. The only thing left to do was to clean up. Once again, Jessica was nowhere to be found.

"I'll make you a deal," Sam said when he saw Elizabeth looking at all the empty soda cans and paper plates. "I'll stay and help you clean up. But you have to do a favor for me."

"If you help me clean up, I'll do anything," Elizabeth said. "Just name it!"

"Go with me to the old house tomorrow," Sam said. "I want someone else to see it."

"I'll be right back," Jessica told Lila. They were up in Jessica's room, reading magazines. Through the window, Jessica could see her sister and Sam cleaning up. She felt a little pang of guilt, but then shrugged it off. After all, Elizabeth had help, didn't she?

She ran down the stairs and into the den. Somewhere in the bookcase was a book about the history of Sweet Valley. Jessica wanted to pick someone out of Sweet Valley history whom she could have been in a past life. Lila wanted everyone to think she used to be Cleopatra, but Jessica would find someone even better.

She searched determinedly through all the book titles until she found the right one. She opened it and looked through the table of contents. A section called "Notorious Women of Sweet Valley" caught her eye. That looked good!

Jessica's smile grew wider and wider as she read further into the section. "This is great!" she whispered, flipping quickly through the pages. Her eyes sparkled with mischief.

Now all she had to do was tell Elizabeth what to say, and Jessica would be ready to put her plan into action!

Five

Jessica waited until her digital clock said 12:30 A.M. From the sound of Lila's breathing, she was sure her friend was asleep in her sleeping bag on the floor of Jessica's room. Now it was time for Jessica to get to work.

"I have to get it back," she muttered in a low voice. To be sure Lila heard her, she thumped her heel on the floor. "I have to get it back," she said again.

"Wha—what?" Lila asked sleepily.

"They wanted to steal my gold," Jessica mumbled. "I had to hide it."

Lila sat up in her sleeping bag. "What are you talking about, Jessica?" she said in a grumpy voice.

Jessica kept her eyes shut. She tossed around

restlessly. "They're coming—but it's *my* gold! It's my gold mine."

"Jessica, are you having a dream?" Lila asked in surprise.

The bathroom door opened and Elizabeth tiptoed in, just the way Jessica had planned.

"What's wrong?" Elizabeth whispered.

Lila unzipped her sleeping bag. "I don't know. Jessica is having some kind of dream and she won't wake up."

"Is she talking about a gold mine?" Elizabeth asked in a frightened tone.

"Yes! How did you know?" Lila gasped.

Jessica moved her head from side to side. "I knew I shouldn't come back to Sweet Valley! I knew they would find me here!" She let out a heavy sigh.

Lila switched on the light. "Wake up, Jessica. What are you talking about?"

"No, don't," Elizabeth cut in quickly. "She does this sometimes, and she just has to wake up by herself. Really, Lila, don't try to wake her up."

More than anything, Jessica wished she could see the expression on Lila's face. But she kept her eyes shut.

"What do you mean?" Lila asked. "She's talking about gold and stuff!"

Elizabeth paused. "Well . . . it's . . . I don't think I should tell you."

"Tell me! Please, Elizabeth!" Lila begged. "I never knew she did this! It's weird!"

"Well, it's just that sometimes it seems like Jessica knows about something that happened a long time ago. I don't want to talk about it anymore. It's so creepy!"

"Do you think she's . . ." Lila trailed off. She sounded excited.

"I'm going back to bed," Elizabeth said. She left the room and shut the door.

Jessica could tell Lila was leaning over her. She let out a troubled sigh.

"Jessica?" Lila whispered. "Can you hear me?"

"Lillian. My name—Lillian Barnes," Jessica moaned.

"Who?" Lila was so excited she reached out and shook Jessica's shoulder gently.

With a gasp, Jessica sat up and stared at Lila. "What is it?"

Lila was looking at her with wide eyes. "You were saying some really strange things," she said.

"What do you mean?" Jessica asked innocently. She pretended to yawn.

Lila bit her lip. "You said your name was Lillian Barnes."

"What?" Jessica laughed and shook her head. "It must have been a dream. But I wonder why I said that name? I've never heard it before."

"She's someone from Sweet Valley. I know I've heard of her," Lila said seriously. "And you said something about gold."

"Gold?" Jessica repeated. She laughed again. "It was a dream, Lila."

"But—" Lila broke off. "Don't you have one of those books about Sweet Valley history?"

Jessica couldn't believe it. Lila was falling right into the trap! Jessica had a hard time keeping a straight face.

"I think my dad has one in the den," she said. "Hey, where are you going?"

Lila was tiptoeing to the door. "I think you might have been Lillian Barnes in a past life, Jessica," Lila said breathlessly. "Let's go see who she was."

"But I don't believe in that stuff," Jessica protested as she followed Lila down the dark hallway.

They crept down the stairs. When they reached the den, Jessica switched on the light. They both blinked.

"I think it's around here somewhere," Jessica said. She pretended to search for the book, even though she knew exactly where it was. Finally she said, "Here it is."

"Let me see." Lila grabbed the book from Jessica and quickly turned to the index. "Look! Barnes, Lillian, page fifty-three!"

Jessica waited while her friend flipped through the pages.

"Here it is," Lila whispered. "Lillian Barnes owned a gold mine near San Francisco in 1850, but two guys tried to steal it from her. She took four boxes of gold nuggets and came to Sweet Valley, where she had been born. They found her and shot her!" Lila's eyes were huge. "But they never found the gold!"

Jessica sat down on the couch. "So what? What's the big deal?" she said, trying to sound bored and sleepy.

Lila closed the book and gulped. "If you were Lillian Barnes in a past life, maybe you know where the gold is!"

"But Lila . . ." Jessica looked thoughtful for a moment. Then she looked scared. "Do you think I'm reincarnated? Really? From someone was got murdered?"

Very slowly, Lila nodded. "I know it's creepy. But if it's true, you could be a millionaire!" she said with awe in her voice. If there was one thing Lila Fowler respected, it was money. The more you had, the more impressed she was. She looked at Jessica with real admiration.

"What do you think I should do?" Jessica asked.

"What else?" Lila declared. "We have to find it!"

Lila left after breakfast the next morning. Elizabeth ran up to her twin sister's room and burst in through the door.

"Did she believe it?" Elizabeth asked breathlessly.

Jessica was trying a new hairstyle, a ponytail on the very top of her head. "She fell right into my trap," she said, giggling.

Elizabeth grinned. "So what did she say when you told her it was a joke?"

"Well . . ." Jessica looked at herself in the mirror and shook her ponytail back and forth. "I didn't exactly tell her yet."

"What?" Elizabeth's eyebrows shot up. "Why not?"

Jessica shrugged. "I don't know. I guess I want to keep teasing her for a little while longer."

"But I don't think—" Elizabeth began. It didn't seem right to trick Lila into believing Jessica was reincarnated.

"Don't worry about it, Lizzie," Jessica said breezily. "I'll tell her."

Elizabeth frowned. "Maybe you shouldn't joke about things like that. Sam really thinks he might be reincarnated."

"Do you believe him?" Jessica asked in surprise.

"I don't know," Elizabeth admitted. "He's pretty serious about it. He wants me to come look at an old house with him today. He's sure he's seen it before."

It was Jessica's turn to frown. "But he just moved here."

"I know. You can come with us if you want, as long as you promise not to tease him. I'm sure Sam won't mind. Will you come?"

Jessica removed the elastic band holding up her ponytail and her hair fell back down onto her shoulders. She paused for a moment and then agreed to go along. "And I promise I'll be nice, don't worry."

Elizabeth looked at her twin. With Jessica, it was impossible *not* to worry!

Six

"Sam! Telephone for you!" Mrs. Sloane called.

Sam's heart sank. He was just about to leave the house. *It's probably Elizabeth*, he thought, *backing out of coming with me.*

He hurried to pick up the kitchen phone. "Hello?"

"Hi," a friendly voice said. "It's Ken Matthews. A bunch of us are going to play some basketball in the park. Do you want to come?"

Basketball? It sounded great to Sam, especially since it meant he was starting to make some friends. He remembered Ken from the party the day before and thought he was really nice. Sam wanted to say yes, but he couldn't. Something was stopping him—the old house on the other side of town.

"Uh, I can't come today," Sam said. "There's something I have to do." It almost hurt him to say it. "But maybe next time, if that's OK."

"OK. Next time," Ken said, and then hung up.

Sam went outside and walked to the corner where he was supposed to meet Elizabeth. He was miserable. *Why am I giving up making friends and playing basketball so that I can go to a stupid old house?* he asked himself. He didn't know why, but somehow that old house was drawing him, and it was a pull he couldn't resist.

He walked to the corner as fast as he could. When he got there, he found both Wakefield twins waiting for him.

"Hi, Sam," Jessica said, giving him a big smile.

"Hi—Jessica," Sam said carefully. "Right?"

"Right," Jessica said.

"I hope you don't mind that I asked Jessica to join us," Elizabeth said.

"I'm glad you're both here," Sam reassured her. "Follow me." The three of them walked for several blocks. Sam didn't say a word. Elizabeth thought he seemed very sad, and she exchanged a nervous look with her twin.

Jessica cleared her throat. "So, Sam, how do you like Sweet Valley so far?"

"I really miss San Francisco," Sam said quickly. "But I'm glad I'm here. I guess that must sound crazy after what I told you, but I really believe that I was meant to come back here for some reason."

"What do you mean, come back?" Elizabeth asked.

"Didn't I tell you?" Sam asked. "I was born here."

"No," Jessica said, with a quick shake of her head. "When did you move away?"

"When I was a baby. My parents died in a car accident—my natural parents, I mean," Sam explained. "I'm adopted. My name used to be Sam Burroughs, and my mom and dad are buried here in Sweet Valley. I don't know where, though."

Elizabeth and Jessica were quiet for a second, thinking this over. "You know what?" Elizabeth finally said. "I don't think the strange feelings you've been having have anything to do with reincarnation."

"Why not?" he asked.

"I don't think you lived in that house in a previous life," Elizabeth said. "I think maybe you lived there in *this* life."

Sam and the twins caught the bus just as it pulled up to the stop.

"You mean, that's where my parents lived before the accident?" Sam said after they had gotten settled in their seats. "That was my home?" The idea seemed to make him happy.

He sat quietly for the rest of the ride, smiling to himself.

They had gotten off the bus and gone a few blocks toward the old house when Sam suddenly stopped walking. "Do you feel that?" he whispered.

Looking at the expression on Sam's face made Elizabeth shiver. He looked scared—very scared.

"Feel what?" she asked carefully.

Sam rubbed his hands together. "It's getting cold," he said.

"No it's not," Elizabeth said gently.

"I'm not cold at all," Jessica said.

Sam frowned. "I guess it's because we're getting near the house," he said at last. They walked the rest of the way in silence. Elizabeth felt a little hesitant.

At the end of the next block they came to McClarendon Street. Without a word, Sam led the way to the middle of the block and pointed to the run-down gray house. A breeze made the tall brown weeds sway back and forth behind the iron fence.

"It's spooky," Jessica whispered.

"Whose house is it?" Elizabeth asked.

"I don't know," Sam said. He fell silent again.

Elizabeth shifted her weight from one foot to the other. She wasn't quite sure what they should do next. She glanced at Sam out of the corner of her eye. He was watching the house intently, as if he were waiting for something to happen. Elizabeth turned her attention back to the house and looked for something out of the ordinary. She saw a sad-looking gray house and nothing more.

"Hey, look! Something moved in that up-stairs window, the open one," Sam cried.

"I didn't see anything," Elizabeth said.

"Me neither," Jessica said. Elizabeth thought she sounded a little disappointed.

"Keep watching," Sam said.

Sam, Jessica, and Elizabeth watched the right corner window in the front of the house. Its glass was gone, leaving just a dark hole behind it.

After a few more minutes, Elizabeth spoke up. "There's nothing there."

"You think I'm making it up, don't you?" Sam asked.

"I believe that you *think* you saw some-thing," Elizabeth said calmly. "But, no, I don't think anything is there."

Sam shook his head. "I saw something," he said stubbornly.

"Well," Elizabeth began with a sigh, "there's only one way to prove nothing's in there."

"You don't mean you're going inside!" Jes-sica said, alarm in her voice. Sam turned to Elizabeth, wide-eyed.

"I meant we should ask the neighbors," Elizabeth said. "They'll probably tell us everything we want to know." She led the way to the porch of one of the houses next door and rang the doorbell.

"Who's out there?" a man's voice called a moment later.

"My name is Elizabeth Wakefield," Elizabeth called back. "Could I talk to you, please?"

"I don't know you. Go away," the man said.

Elizabeth shrugged.

"Come on," Jessica said. "I'll knock at the next one." They went to the house on the other side of the old mansion and Jessica knocked on the door. It was answered by a middle-aged woman in a brightly colored dress.

"We'd like to ask you a question," Jessica told her in her most polite voice. "If you don't mind."

"Ask away," the woman said with a smile.

"This is our friend, Sam," Jessica began. "He used to live in Sweet Valley when he was a baby, and he was wondering if maybe he used to live in the house next door."

"What's your last name, Sam?" the woman said.

"Sloane, but my name used to be Burroughs."

Sam was hoping he would finally find out why the old house was so important to him. But the woman shook her head.

"That's old man Seever's house," the woman said.

"Oh," Sam said glumly.

"Who's he?" Jessica asked.

"Jeremiah Seever was a very rich old man," the woman said. "Not that you could tell it from looking at his house."

"It's not in very good shape. Has it been empty long?" Jessica asked.

"Mr. Seever died a couple of months ago. But I'll tell you something, it looked just as bad when he was alive. He lived by himself and never spent a nickel without an argument. Believe it or not, sometimes he wouldn't come out for weeks."

"That's sad," Elizabeth said.

The woman shrugged her shoulders. "Well, he wasn't the nicest person in the neighborhood. He never had a pleasant thing to say to anyone. Perhaps if he had been a little more friendly he wouldn't have been so lonely."

"What's going to happen to the house?" Sam asked the woman.

"If they can't find an heir, the town council will probably sell it—to a developer, I'd guess."

"Well, thanks," Elizabeth said after a pause.

"You're welcome," the woman answered. After she had gone back inside, Sam turned and walked off the porch. Jessica and Elizabeth had to hurry to catch up with him.

"Where are you going, Sam?" Jessica asked.

Sam didn't answer her. He walked over to the Seever mansion and grabbed two bars of the iron fence. He pulled on them, trying to open the gate, but it was locked.

Elizabeth came up to stand beside Sam. "I'm sorry this wasn't your house," she said softly.

"It's not your fault," Sam said without looking at her. He stood there, staring at the old, empty house.

"What do you want to do now, Sam?" Jessica asked.

Sam was quiet for a minute. "I think I'd like to be alone for a while," he said at last. "I have a lot of thinking to do. Would you mind taking the bus back without me?"

"Come on, Lizzie. Let's go," Jessica said quietly.

"OK, we'll see you later," Elizabeth told Sam.

Sam didn't reply. He just kept staring at the house until they were gone.

With his hands grasping the fence's iron posts, Sam closed his eyes. He tried as hard as he could to find his earliest memory, to find a place for this house in his past. But it was hopeless. He couldn't remember his natural parents, and he couldn't remember the house. Before he had come to Sweet Valley, his past hadn't ever really meant anything to him. It was only a story his parents told him. He still couldn't really *remember* anything. But every place he went and everything he saw seemed as familiar to him as if he had known about it his entire life.

Sam opened his eyes and noticed that it was starting to get dark. He knew he should be heading home for dinner, but there was someplace he had to go first. He knew exactly where it was, although he had never been there before. And he knew exactly what he would find there.

Seven

◇

Sam walked faster and faster, until he was almost running. He knew that soon it would be too dark to see the street signs. Not that Sam needed them. He knew how to get where he was going. By now he was so used to this feeling that it almost didn't bother him anymore.

"Whyte Memorial Cemetery," Sam read aloud from a large printed sign that hung on a tall, rusty iron gate. No one was nearby, and his own breathing sounded very loud to him. He took a deep breath and squeezed through a small opening in the gate.

For a moment he simply stood looking around. The cemetery spread out as far as he could see. In every direction, Sam saw straight rows of gravestones.

This is crazy, Sam thought. *I can't find my parents' graves in the dark.* He noticed the sky had turned from pink to purple.

Suddenly a hand grabbed Sam from behind —grabbed him hard. Sam wanted to scream, but his throat instantly tightened up and he couldn't. Before he could run, the hand turned him around. He found himself looking into the piercing eyes of a tall, gaunt, angry-looking man.

"You!" the man growled, looking at Sam with one eye open and one eye squinting. "What are you doing here, boy?"

Sam was so frightened, he couldn't say anything. The grip on his shoulder tightened.

"Nobody comes *visiting* at this hour. What've you got, boy? A can of spray paint? A hammer?"

Sam's heart was pounding so hard he thought he would burst.

"I don't like kids who sneak in here and tear the place up." The man's hand squeezed Sam's shoulder even harder. "What kind of mischief did you bring, boy?"

"I—I—I'm looking for my parents' graves," Sam finally said.

"Sure, boy. What're their names?"

"Burroughs," Sam said, trying to squirm away.

"I've got lots of Burroughs here. Tell me their full names."

"I don't know!" Sam shouted, almost in tears. "I never knew my parents' first names."

The man was silent. The wind made a strange whistling noise as it swirled around the graves.

Finally the man let go of Sam's shoulder. "What are you talking about?" he asked more gently.

"My parents died when I was a baby," Sam explained. "I've never been here before."

"How do you know they're here?"

"Because I know," Sam said. "I just know."

"I know everyone who's come in here the last thirty years. I buried them all. My name's Clayton. I'm the caretaker." The man stretched out his large, strong hand again, but this time it was to shake Sam's hand.

"I'm Sam," Sam said.

"So many kids come here to cause mischief," Clayton said, shaking his head. "I think it's because they're scared. Are you scared of this place, Sam?"

Sam looked straight at Clayton. "Yes," he said.

Clayton chuckled and said, "It's not scary. Sometimes dead people are a lot friendlier than the living. When did your parents die? I can find their graves for you." Clayton pointed to his head. "I've got a map of this whole place up here."

"I'll find them myself," Sam said.

Clayton cocked his head and looked up at the sky. "It'll be dark soon," he said.

Sam zipped up his jacket and put his hands in his pockets. "I know."

"If you get lost, just yell *Clayton!* I hear people calling my name around here all the time, especially at night." He chuckled again and walked away.

Sam stood still. He took his wallet out of his back pocket and removed a folded photograph from inside. While there was still some light, he looked closely at the picture. It was the only one he had of his natural parents.

Sam's father had been tall, with a big build. He had had a full beard, and in the photo he was grinning broadly. His mother had been pretty and small with curly dark hair, like Sam's. The picture showed Sam's mother and father standing on a beach with their arms around each other's waists. Off to one side there was a volleyball net and some other people wearing swimsuits.

They looked so happy. Sam quickly put the photograph back in his wallet. He realized that he was afraid to see his parents' graves. When he did, they would no longer be the same happy people he saw standing on the beach. They'd really be dead.

Sam turned, sensing which way was the right direction. He slowly walked toward a row of graves with low markers. His throat was tightening up, and he swallowed hard. Sam could feel that he was close. He took a few more steps, and then stopped. He looked down at the inscriptions on the gravestones.

Theodore Burroughs. Next to it was a marker with the name Julie Burroughs. The gravestones said they had been born in the same year and had died on the same day.

Sam read the inscriptions over and over. Then he looked around and noticed the names on some of the other gravestones. He walked over to them.

Barbara Randolph Burroughs. Harriet Burroughs. Zena Smithers Burroughs. For the first time Sam realized he used to have a lot of relatives and that they had all lived right here in Sweet Valley. He felt happy, alone, and confused, all at once.

There was one more grave with the name Burroughs. Sam could make out the name Michael Burroughs in the dim light. He studied the marker, which was inscribed with the year of Michael's birth and death. Michael Burroughs had died thirty years ago. He'd been just a kid when he died—only eleven years old. That was Sam's age also. He wondered about Michael Burroughs. What did he look like? When was his birthday? Was he good at sports?

Sam suddenly became aware of the sound of footsteps approaching him. He had been so intent on the graves that he hadn't been paying attention to anything else around him. Suddenly, Sam felt a pang of terror. The footsteps seemed to come from all directions at once. Who would be in the cemetery so late?

"Who's there?" Sam asked.

The footsteps stopped, as if they were afraid of Sam's voice. But then they started again. They got louder and closer.

"Clayton?" Sam called.

The footsteps stopped again.

Sam turned in a complete circle, straining his eyes to see in the misty dusk.

The footsteps started again. Sam clenched his fists tightly.

Now he could tell that the sound was coming from behind him. Sam whirled. Was that a shadow? No, someone was walking toward him.

Sam caught his breath and held it so long, he started to feel dizzy. He couldn't believe what he was seeing. A figure about his size was coming toward him. *No!* Sam told himself. It was too unbelievable. It was a *ghost!* It was a ghost with *Sam's* face!

Sam looked away for a second and glanced at the grave of Michael Burroughs. Then he looked up again. The ghost was still standing there. Was it the ghost of Michael Burroughs?

Sam couldn't stand it a second longer. He took off, running through the cemetery as fast as he could.

Eight

◇

Elizabeth was sitting in the Sweet Valley library. A book was open on the table in front of her. She thumbed through *The Story of Reincarnation*. The whole idea seemed crazy to her, but lots of famous people had believed in it: Henry Ford, Napoleon, and even Benjamin Franklin. They had really believed they would come back after death and continue with the same spirit in another body.

Elizabeth found it hard to believe that Sam could know about things in Sweet Valley before he ever saw them. But he didn't seem like the type of person to lie. And when Elizabeth remembered his face as they had walked to the old house, she knew Sam had been genuinely afraid of something.

Elizabeth felt goosebumps rise on her arms. What if Sam really *was* telling the truth? Deep down, Elizabeth thought that it was impossible, but she couldn't think of any other explanation for the strange feelings Sam had been having. Finally she gathered up her things and started out the door.

When Elizabeth got outside, she sensed something strange in the air—something that made her wish she hadn't stayed out quite so late. *Is Sam still at the old house?* she wondered. *What a creepy place to be—especially after dark.*

"Elizabeth?"

Elizabeth froze. She was certain nobody had been in front of the library when she had come out. She peered into the darkness, trying to guess where the voice was coming from.

"Elizabeth? Is that you?"

Elizabeth felt someone tap her shoulder from behind, and she whirled around. "Sam!" Elizabeth said with relief. "You frightened me! What are you *doing* here?" Then Elizabeth noticed the strange look on Sam's face. "What's wrong?" she asked.

"You probably won't believe this, but I just saw a ghost!" Sam told her.

"A ghost?" Elizabeth repeated.

"Yes. I saw it in the cemetery. I went there to find my parents' graves," Sam replied.

"You did? How did you find them?" Elizabeth asked.

"I just knew where they would be, that's all. My mother and father are buried side by side. And a lot of other relatives are there, too. They've all got my old last name, Burroughs. One of them was a boy named Michael, and he died when he was my age, eleven. I think it was his ghost that I saw. I really did see a ghost!" Sam insisted.

He was talking so fast, Elizabeth could hardly understand it all.

"What did he look like?" she asked.

"Are you ready for this?" Sam said. "He looked exactly like me. He had *my* face. We just stared at each other. Maybe he was going to tell me something, but I got scared and ran."

Sam took a deep breath. Then he noticed the doubtful expression on Elizabeth's face. "OK. You don't believe me. You know what? I don't blame you! I wouldn't believe me, either. But I can prove it! Come to the cemetery with me, and I'll show you."

"Now?" Elizabeth said. "It's too dark. I've got to go home."

"How about tomorrow afternoon?" Sam asked.

"OK," Elizabeth agreed slowly.

"Great!" Sam said.

"I know you saw something, Sam," Elizabeth said.

"I didn't just see *something*. I saw a *ghost*," he declared.

*   *   *

Twenty minutes later, Elizabeth hurried in through the back door of the Wakefields' house.

Jessica was sitting on one of the kitchen counters talking on the phone. Elizabeth signaled to her to hurry up. As soon as her sister hung up, Elizabeth said, "Guess what? Sam thinks he saw a ghost."

Jessica's eyes opened wide. "Sam saw a *what?*"

"I just ran into Sam at the library," Elizabeth began.

"He called while I was at Lila's," Jessica interrupted her. "Mom told him you were there."

"Oh," Elizabeth said, "I wondered about that. Anyway, he went to the cemetery after we left him. He found his parents' graves. And he thinks he saw a ghost!"

"Wow," Jessica said. "Do you believe him, Lizzie? I mean, do you believe in ghosts?"

"No, I don't. But Sam obviously saw something out there. I told him I'd go with him to the cemetery tomorrow to see if it'll appear again. I want you to come with us."

Jessica's mouth dropped open. "Well, I—" she began.

"Come on, Jess. You're not afraid of an imaginary ghost, are you?" Elizabeth asked with a grin.

"I don't know . . ." Jessica's voice trailed off. "Something weird is going on around here, Elizabeth," she said seriously.

Elizabeth nodded in silent agreement. "I know," she said. "And that's why we have to go with him to the cemetery tomorrow afternoon. To find out exactly what it is."

"OK," Jessica agreed solemnly. "I promise I'll go."

The next morning, Jessica waited for Lila on the library steps.

Lila came riding up on her new bike. She looked excited. "Hi, Jessica!" she panted.

"Hi," Jessica replied, jumping to her feet.

"Listen, I've been thinking," Lila announced as they went up the steps. "Let's not tell anyone else about you being the reincarnation of Lillian Barnes, OK?" She looked at Jessica hopefully. "Don't even tell the other Unicorns."

Jessica grinned. Lila wanted the gold to herself! "OK," she agreed. "But I still can't figure out how we're going to find it."

"That's why I told you to meet me here," Lila explained quickly. "I could hypnotize you! We'll find a book that tells us how to do it!"

Jessica gulped. What if Lila really did hypnotize her? She might say something that would give the joke away! But Jessica didn't think just anyone could be a hypnotist, especially Lila. She tried not to worry.

"All right," Jessica said bravely.

They went into the library and searched through the card catalog. There were three books about hypnotism, and Lila brought all of them to a table in the reading room.

"Here's what you do," Lila began, frowning at the first page of *Beginning Hypnotism.* "Empty your mind."

Jessica made a face. "How?"

"I don't know how, just do it," her friend said impatiently.

"OK." Jessica stared into space and crossed her eyes. "It's empty."

"Good. Now concentrate on the sound of my voice," Lila commanded. "Your eyes are getting heavy. You are feeling very tired."

Jessica wanted to giggle, but she held it back. She began to blink her eyes slowly.

"Lillian Barnes? Are you there?" Lila whispered.

Jessica closed her eyes. "Yes?" she answered in a faraway voice.

"Where do you live?" Lila asked. "Do you live in Sweet Valley?"

Jessica searched her mind for a good answer. Then she had a brilliant idea!

"Yes, on—McClarendon Street," she said hesitantly. She nodded once. "McClarendon Street."

"Is that where you hid the gold?" Lila said eagerly.

"Shh!" A woman hissed at them from another table. "This is a library, girls!"

Jessica snapped her eyes open. "Did I say anything?"

"McClarendon Street," Lila replied with a happy smile. "Let's go!"

Fifteen minutes later, Jessica and Lila turned their bikes onto McClarendon Street. Jessica saw the ramshackle old house that fascinated Sam.

"Hey," she said, slowing down. "This really looks familiar for some reason."

"What?" Lila gasped. "Do you see something?" She looked around at all the big houses.

Instead of answering, Jessica let her bike roll to a stop in front of the spooky old mansion. Lila braked and let out a whistle. "Is this it?" she whispered. "Have you been here before?"

"Yes," Jessica answered truthfully. She looked up at the house. Sam said he had seen something in one of the broken windows. The overgrown weeds swayed in the yard. It seemed to be darker there than anywhere else on the street. Jessica began to feel uncomfortable.

"Listen, I don't want to go in there," she said nervously.

Lila looked surprised. "Why not? Isn't it the right place?"

"No, I was wrong," Jessica said. She hopped back on her bike. "We're supposed to meet the rest of the Unicorns at Casey's Place now, anyway."

Lila let out a heavy sigh. "Oh, right. OK. But remember, don't tell the others."

"I won't," Jessica agreed quickly. The sooner they left McClarendon Street, the better she would feel.

"Maybe he didn't really go to the cemetery," Tamara Chase said. The Unicorns were eating ice cream sundaes at Casey's Place, one of the club's favorite hangouts. Jessica had just told them about Sam and the ghost in the cemetery, but she didn't say anything about the creepy old house.

"I don't believe he saw a ghost," Ellen added.

"Well, *I* believe him," Lila said.

"Do you believe in ghosts, Lila?" Ellen asked.

"Yes, I do," Lila said firmly. "I've seen one."

By then, Lila had the full attention of all of the Unicorns.

"When?" Jessica asked.

"Where?" Ellen asked at the same time. She exchanged glances with Jessica and both girls giggled.

Lila smiled mysteriously. "It was last summer, when my father and I were vacationing in

Milan. That's in Italy. We rented an old villa, probably about two hundred years old. The place was enormous and my bedroom was as big as the cafeteria at school. It was at the top of a long marble staircase." Lila paused to take a mouthful of ice cream.

"Go on, Lila," Ellen encouraged her. "I can't stand the suspense."

"Oh, sorry," Lila said calmly. "Well, at first I didn't see the ghost, but I started noticing that things were out of place. One of my hairbrushes wouldn't be with the others. One of my nightgowns would be in the wrong drawer. Then one night I heard someone laughing. I looked in the hallway outside my room and on my balcony, but no one was there. The more I looked, the louder the laughing got. I must have searched for hours, but I never found out where the laughter was coming from.

"The next night, the laughing started again right before I fell asleep. This time, I just sat on my bed and said, 'What's so funny?' "

"Weren't you scared?" Ellen demanded.

"Shh!" Several of the girls quieted her.

"That's when I saw him," Lila continued. "He was floating up near the ceiling. I could see him perfectly and see through him at the same time. He said that a hundred years ago he had been murdered in that very same room. His brother stabbed him to death just before the clock struck midnight. Because he couldn't sleep peacefully in that room, he saw to it that no one else did, either. He killed everyone who came to sleep in that room."

"Gross," Tamara commented.

"What did you do?" Ellen asked.

"I had the servants move my things into another bedroom, of course," Lila said. "The villa had twenty-three bedrooms, so there was no reason to stay there."

Tamara turned to Lila. "Did you just make that up?" she challenged.

Jessica watched carefully for the smallest hint of a smile, which always meant that her friend was telling a story. If Lila really believed in ghosts, that would explain why she believed Jessica was reincarnated.

Lila didn't smile. "I'll give you my father's private office number and you can call him yourself," Lila said.

"That's OK. I believe you," Tamara said quickly.

Jessica sat listening with a lump in her throat. She couldn't stop thinking about where she was going later that afternoon—to the graveyard with Elizabeth and Sam! Suddenly Jessica felt as if she couldn't eat another bite. What if Sam really had seen a ghost in the cemetery? And what if it came back that very afternoon, while she was there? Even if she had told Elizabeth she'd go, there was no way she was going to let a ghost get her.

"I have to go home," she announced right in the middle of a story Ellen was telling.

Her friends looked at her in surprise. "Right now?" Lila asked.

"Yes. I just remembered something I have to do—immediately," Jessica said, sliding out of the booth. "Bye."

She hurried out of Casey's Place and jumped on her bike. She had to convince Elizabeth to go to the cemetery without her. As she rode, she kept imagining gravestones covered with cobwebs and pale, moaning ghosts with rusty chains. She wasn't sure exactly what a ghost would do if it caught her, but she didn't want to find out.

"Lizzie?" Jessica called out as soon as she got in the door. The house seemed very quiet. She ran up the stairs to her sister's bedroom. "Lizzie? Are you here?"

Elizabeth was lying on her stomach on the bed, reading. "Hi, Jess."

"I'm so glad you're here!" Jessica gasped, leaning against the doorframe.

"Where did you think I would be?" Elizabeth asked with a little laugh.

Jessica caught her breath. "Oh, I don't know. Listen," she began, sitting down next to her sister. "About this afternoon?" Elizabeth was silent. "You know, going to the cemetery?" Jessica went on. She tried to give Elizabeth her most coaxing look.

"What about it?" Elizabeth asked. She sounded suspicious.

"Well, it's just that . . . I remembered I was supposed to do something else," Jessica mumbled. She couldn't quite meet her sister's eyes.

Elizabeth sat up. "What were you supposed to do?"

"Oh, um, I was going to—to rearrange my closet," Jessica explained.

"But you promised to go to the cemetery with me and Sam!" Elizabeth exclaimed. "Why can't you rearrange your closet tomorrow? It's been a mess for a long time. It can wait another day."

"I know, but—" Jessica began.

"Don't try to get out of it, Jessica," Elizabeth said firmly. "You made a promise, remember?"

"But—"

"Sam is really counting on us," Elizabeth went on. "He doesn't know very many people yet, and he's going through a difficult time right now."

"But—" Jessica twisted the hem of her shirt between her fingers. "I don't know why Sam wants to go to a creepy old cemetery anyway."

Elizabeth looked upset. "Because weird things have been happening and he has to find out what's going on," she said. "We're really the only friends he has, and we have to be there to help."

"But it's a graveyard, Lizzie!" Jessica wailed.

"Did someone say graveyard?" asked a voice in the hall. Steven stood in the doorway, looking from Jessica to Elizabeth expectantly.

The twins stared at him. "What do you want, Steven?" Elizabeth asked coolly.

"Yeah," Jessica said. "We're having a private conversation, if you don't mind."

Steven put his hands in his pockets. "I just thought I'd let you know what I heard about the graveyard, but if you're not interested, fine." He turned and started to walk away.

Jessica gulped. Maybe what he had to say was important. "What about it?" she called after him.

Steven came back, and took a few steps into Elizabeth's room.

"Well, these two guys in ninth grade—Mark Pastor and Derek Miller—dared each other to spend the whole night in the graveyard. And they did it!"

"Well?" Jessica prompted him.

Steven looked solemn. "Some *really* strange things happened while they were there."

"What things?" Elizabeth asked.

"Noises," Steven said dramatically. "Very strange noises. Coming from *under the ground*."

Jessica's stomach flipflopped. "You mean, like from the dead people?"

"I don't believe it," Elizabeth said calmly. "You're just making that up to scare us!"

"Hey, I'm just telling you what I heard," Steven said with a shrug. "If you don't want to know what else goes on there, that's fine with me."

"You mean there's something else?" Jessica asked. "Besides the—noises?"

Their brother glanced out into the hall for a moment, and then dropped his voice. "It was too dark to see anything really clearly, but they said they could see shapes. Black shapes, moving all over the graveyard."

"Really?" Jessica asked in a tiny voice.

"Really," Steven repeated seriously. He crossed his heart and snapped his fingers twice. That was the promise signal they had all used when they were little. "That's what they said."

Jessica turned to look at her sister. "Listen, Lizzie," Jessica pleaded. "Do you *still* think we should go?"

"I think Steven's friends just made that up," Elizabeth said firmly. "I bet they wanted everyone to think they were really brave because they stayed in the cemetery all night. They probably didn't even stay past dark."

Steven looked serious. "You could be right, Elizabeth," he said. "But then again, you could be wrong." He strolled away down the hall to his room. A few seconds later, Jessica and Elizabeth heard his bedroom door shut.

Jessica let her breath out all at once and glanced at Elizabeth. "I don't believe him," she said faintly.

"Me neither," Elizabeth agreed. She laughed. "Come on, Jess. Graveyards are perfectly ordinary. There's no reason to believe everyone who's buried there is a creepy monster that comes out at night and tries to get you."

"Right," Jessica said, nodding. "I guess I don't really mind going with Sam. There's probably just a perfectly normal, simple explanation for what he saw."

Elizabeth stood up. "I know there is. So let's go," she said, walking out of the room.

"Right. Let's go." Jessica stood up, too, but she didn't follow her sister. What if Steven *wasn't* joking? What if Sam really *had* seen a ghost? Jessica shivered.

"Jessica, are you coming?" Elizabeth called impatiently from downstairs.

"I'm coming, Lizzie!" Jessica took a deep breath and left the room. "There's no such thing as ghosts," she muttered under her breath as she raced down the stairs, but it didn't make her feel better. What had she let Elizabeth talk her into?

Nine

◇

Sam fidgeted nervously. He and the Wakefield twins had been standing in the cemetery for half an hour, waiting.

"It's so quiet here," Jessica whispered, "it makes me want to scream!"

Elizabeth smiled at her sister, but Sam thought she looked a little impatient, too.

Sam knelt in the grass in front of a grave that was covered with flowers. He tightened his shoelace for about the tenth time.

Elizabeth looked at her watch. "I hate to say this, Sam, but I'm afraid your ghost isn't going to show up."

"Why are you sorry?" Jessica asked. "We don't *actually* want to see a ghost, you know!"

Just then a wet, chilly breeze blew into the graveyard. Sam felt as if he were being watched.

"Hey, look at that," Sam said, moving to his feet quickly.

"What?" Jessica asked. She sounded scared.

"Those other graves. They must be my relatives, too," Sam said. "I didn't see them last night."

Lillian Burroughs. James Burroughs. Peter Burroughs, Sam read silently. "I wonder what happened to them," he said aloud. Nobody answered him.

"There's Michael's gravestone," Sam told the girls and pointed to the marker. Jessica and Elizabeth nodded.

No matter where Sam looked, he thought he saw something move out of the corner of his eye. *It would be easy to hide behind a gravestone*, he thought.

"Tell me about the ghost," Jessica said. "What did he do? Did you see him float out of his grave and fly in the air? What did he look like?"

"He looked like me," Sam said.

"But ghosts don't look like people," Jessica said.

Sam frowned and turned away. Part of him wanted Elizabeth and Jessica to be there if the ghost came, but part of him wanted to be there alone. After all, something had been making *him* come to the cemetery, not them.

Suddenly a scream pierced the air. Sam spun

around and saw Jessica clutching Elizabeth's arm. She was pointing toward the cemetery gate. Sam followed her gaze. Only fifty yards away the ghost stood frozen.

Sam was staring right into its eyes. The ghost's hair, his face, his expression, everything about him looked exactly like Sam.

"He's going to get us!" Jessica screamed.

The ghost didn't say a word. He just turned and ran away.

Instantly Elizabeth took off after him.

"Lizzie! Come back!" Jessica shouted.

When Elizabeth didn't stop, Sam started to run after her.

"Hey! Wait!" Sam heard Elizabeth shout as she ran to the gate. Soon she was out of the cemetery and running down the street. Sam had to run as fast as he could to keep her in sight. "Hey! Stop! Come on!" Elizabeth called out again.

The ghost stopped.

He turned around and faced Elizabeth. "You look just like Sam!" Elizabeth blurted out as Sam ran up to them.

"Why were you chasing me?" the ghost asked. He looked scared and ready to start running again in an instant.

"Because I knew you weren't a ghost," Elizabeth said. "Ghosts don't wear Johnny Buck T-shirts or have suntans. Who are you?"

"David Barton," he said.

David Barton? For a minute, Sam stood staring at the boy who looked exactly like him. "I don't believe this," he finally said. "Why do you look like me?"

"I don't know," David answered. "Who are you?"

"Sam Sloane."

The two boys stared at each other for a long time. Sam didn't know what to say—and he couldn't shake the feeling that he was looking at a ghost. *How can there be another person in the world who looks just like me?* he wondered. It didn't seem real.

Jessica broke the silence. Sam hadn't even noticed that she had caught up to them.

"I'm Jessica Wakefield, and this is my sister, Elizabeth," she told David. "We're twins and I'll bet you two are, too," she said, turning to include Sam in her comment.

Twins. Sam couldn't think of any other explanation for what he was seeing—an exact duplicate of himself.

"We can't be twins," David protested. "I mean, nobody ever said I had a twin, so—"

"How old are you?" Sam interrupted him.

"Eleven," said David. "Well, twelve next Thursday."

"Then we must be twins," Sam said, "because *I'm* going to be twelve next Thursday, too.''

David's face turned pale.

"I don't believe this," Jessica said excitedly. "This is too fabulous to be true!"

"Is this a joke or something?" David asked.

Sam looked away from David. He looked over toward the cemetery. "There's only one way to find out," he said seriously. "My parents are dead. And they're buried in there. What about yours?"

"Your parents are buried here?" David asked in disbelief. "What's their last name?"

"Burroughs," Sam said.

"Ted and Julie?" David asked.

Sam didn't know whether he should laugh or cry. "Yes, Ted and Julie," he said. "I was adopted when I was nine months old."

"I was adopted, too," David said. "When I was ten months old."

No one talked for a minute. Sam and David seemed to be waiting for someone to tell them what to do. Finally Elizabeth spoke. "I think you guys better go home and talk to your parents."

"I can't believe that I haven't seen you before!" David exclaimed as he, Sam, Jessica, and Elizabeth waited for the bus. Since David's parents would still be at work, the boys had decided to go to Sam's house first.

"I just moved here," Sam explained. "I used to live in San Francisco."

"I've lived in Sweet Valley all my life," David told them.

"You must go to the other school. That must be why we never met," Elizabeth remarked.

"Did your parents ever tell you about me?" Sam asked. David shook his head. *It's unbelievable*, Sam thought. Then it suddenly dawned on him.

"Now I understand!" Sam exclaimed. "You're the reason why that man at the marina recognized me—and you're the reason why everything has seemed so familiar to me! You must have been sending me messages about Sweet Valley!"

"Wow!" Jessica cried. "You mean there's a link between you because you're twins? Sometimes Lizzie and I have that."

"Really?" David said. He sounded interested but not quite convinced.

"It's true," Elizabeth said. "Sometimes when Jess is in trouble, I can sense it. Or sometimes I'll come home from school and Jess will know, before I even say anything, that something bad happened to me that day. It's like ESP."

The four of them talked nonstop the whole time on the bus. Sam noticed that while they talked, passengers were turning around to stare at them. He had to admit they must have made a strange sight—two sets of identical twins!

"Hey, you guys," Elizabeth exclaimed. "This is our stop!" They quickly gathered their things, jumped up, and ran off the bus just as it was about to pull away from the curb.

Elizabeth and Jessica chattered as they walked down the block. They asked David about his family, his neighborhood, and his school. Soon they reached the Wakefields' house, and the girls turned up their front walk, calling goodbye to Sam and David.

After they were gone, the boys walked in silence the rest of the way to Sam's house.

A droopy-eyed St. Bernard came galloping to the front door, barking and wagging his tail, when Sam walked in.

"Hi, Terry," Sam said. "How are you, boy?"

David froze and stood staring at the dog.

"What's wrong?" Sam asked, holding the collar around Terry's neck. "Are you afraid of dogs?"

"No," David said slowly. "Your dog is named Terry . . . and so is mine."

Sam could only stand there in astonishment. **For a brief moment the feeling returned—the** strange feeling he had had ever since he came to Sweet Valley. *But it's over now,* Sam told himself. *I've found David. There's nothing more to worry about.*

Terry wagged his tail wildly, sniffing first one boy and then the other. He seemed to know that David and Sam were twins.

"I think he likes you," Sam said. Then he led the way into the house. "Mom, I'm home," he called out. "And I've brought a friend home with me."

Sam's mother was in the living room talking on the phone. She smiled and waved at Sam as he came in. But when David walked into the room, Mrs. Sloane's face went from happy to surprised to pale in a matter of seconds.

"Randy," she said to her husband over the phone, her voice shaking, "you'd better come home as fast as you can."

When she hung up, Sam and David told her how they met in the cemetery. And then Sam explained how he had found his natural parents' graves.

"Sam, this is amazing," Mrs. Sloane said, shaking her head. "It's incredible. It's . . . it's . . ."

"Yeah, I know, Mom," Sam said.

"I had no idea," Mrs. Sloane continued. "The lawyers told us there was one boy, you, Sam. I just can't believe you have a twin!"

When Sam's father arrived, he found Mrs. Sloane sitting at their kitchen table with the boys.

"What's the emergency?" Mr. Sloane asked his wife.

But before Mrs. Sloane could answer, Sam signaled to his twin to turn around.

"Dad, this is David."

"What on earth?" Sam's father stammered as he looked from Sam to David.

"Better have a seat, Randy," said Mrs. Sloane. "Sam will explain."

Mr. Sloane sat down.

"This is my brother, David," Sam told his father.

"Hello," David said, smiling broadly.

"Your brother?"

"Yeah, isn't it unbelievable, Dad?" Sam said. "And you know where we found each other? At the cemetery where our natural parents are buried."

"We both thought we were seeing a ghost that looked exactly like us," David explained.

"But we didn't know there were two of you," Mr. Sloane said. "This is terrible!"

"It's not terrible, Dad," Sam said. "It's great. It would have been terrible if I'd never found him."

Mr. Sloane nodded. "I just meant it's too

bad you were separated. I wonder how it happened?"

"I don't know, but I'm going to find out," Sam said. "And guess what else? David has a dog whose name is Terry. Do you believe that? If it's OK, I want to go over to David's house in a little while so I can meet his parents."

Mr. Sloane kept looking from one boy to the other, shaking his head. Sam and David laughed at the look of astonishment on his face.

"Is it OK if Sam has dinner at my house?" David asked.

"Sure. Of course!" Mrs. Sloane said.

For the next hour Sam and David talked to Sam's parents. Sam realized that he already felt as if he had known David forever. Just before they left, Sam took David to see his bedroom.

"Hey, cool—Johnny Buck posters," David said, looking around. "I've got them all over my room, too. My dad says they're holding the walls up."

"The Buck is the greatest," Sam said.

"Absolutely!"

Since David's house was on the far side of town, Mr. Sloane gave them a ride there. The boys crept up the driveway, hoping that nobody would see them until they got inside.

"I want to surprise them the way we surprised your mom and dad," David whispered.

When David and Sam walked into the Bartons' house, Mr. and Mrs. Barton were sitting in their living room watching the news on TV. A large dog lay sleeping with its chin on Mr. Barton's foot. *Terry*, Sam thought, and smiled to himself.

David's parents looked at the two boys.

"Sam!" Mrs. Barton cried after a moment of silence. "What are *you* doing here?"

Ten

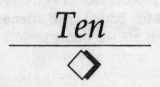

"Mom," David exclaimed, "how did you know Sam's name?"

Mrs. Barton didn't answer, so David gave his father a questioning look.

"Hello, Sam," Mr. Barton said calmly. "We're really happy to see you. Come in. Sit down, please." Mr. Barton put his glasses on the coffee table and leaned forward to turn off the TV. He took a deep breath. "This is most interesting," he finally said. "How did you—"

David quickly told his father the story of how he and Sam had met just a few hours before.

"David, I guess your mother and I should have told you about your brother a long time ago."

Sam sat on the couch, afraid to say anything. He could tell David was upset and hurt.

"You mean you *knew* I had a twin and didn't tell me? How could you do that?"

"Please don't be upset, David. When we tell you the whole story, you'll understand."

"David," Mrs. Barton said, coming to sit on the couch next to her son, "we were going to tell you about Sam—but later, when you were older. When you could do something about it. We didn't want to tell you that you had a brother and then just let you wonder about him and wish that he could be here with you."

"But he *is* here now, Mom. So please tell me what happened. Why were we separated all this time?" David asked angrily.

Mr. Barton leaned forward in his chair. "As you know, David, we had just moved to Sweet Valley when you were born. We didn't know your parents. We heard about the car crash on television and we knew some of the details. You know your mother and your father were in the car. Your grandmother was, too."

"Her name was Lillian Burroughs," Mrs. Barton said.

"She's buried next to James Burroughs in the cemetery," Sam said. "I saw their graves." Sam was finally learning something about his relatives.

"That's right, Sam. James was your grandfather. He died a long time ago, in World War II," Mrs. Barton explained. "When your parents and grandmother were killed, your only close relative was your Great-Aunt Bea, who was our neighbor. She was given custody of both of you. Your great-aunt was very old, and after a little while, she decided—" Mrs. Barton stopped. She gave Mr. Barton a pleading glance.

"She realized she was too old to take care of both of you, and she thought she could manage better if she had only one baby," Mr. Barton continued carefully. "She thought both of you would be better off if she put one of you up for adoption."

"Who did Great-Aunt Bea give up?" David asked. "How could she do something like that?" he added.

"It's very difficult to take care of two infants, David," Mrs. Barton said gently. "It was too much for her. So she decided to put Sam up for adoption."

"I knew it was me," Sam said quietly.

"Sam, it was very hard for your Great-Aunt Bea to give you up," Mrs. Barton said. "She told us so later. But she felt she didn't have a choice. Your great-aunt hired a lawyer to handle your adoption. She was afraid that if the people who adopted you knew you had a twin, they'd want to adopt him, too. She couldn't bear the thought of losing both of you, so she decided to keep

David's existence a secret. She never told the lawyers about him, and she instructed them never to mention her name to Sam's new parents. Mr. and Mrs. Sloane never knew she existed. Just a week after Sam had been adopted, your Great-Aunt Bea fell and broke her hip. Her doctors told her she might be in bed recovering for as long as a year. So your great-aunt had to admit that she was too old to be a good mother even to the one baby she had kept—you, David. She decided to put you up for adoption, too. We were the lucky people who got you."

"Why didn't you adopt Sam, too?" David asked.

"Sweetheart, we would have," Mrs. Barton said. "We wanted to, but we just couldn't."

"David," his father explained, "we knew that Sam had been adopted by people who loved him very much and that they would have been terribly hurt if we had tried to take him away from them. But even if we had decided to find Sam it would have been impossible. Your Great-Aunt Bea didn't know who had adopted him because the lawyers weren't allowed to tell her. We decided it was best to leave the situation alone."

"I'm glad," Sam told them. "My mom and dad are great."

"This feels like a miracle of some kind," Mrs. Barton said, "seeing the two of you sitting there next to each other."

"Sam and I have a lot to talk about," David said. He still sounded a little angry. "Can he sleep over tonight?"

"If it's OK with his parents," Mr. Barton said.

"As a matter of fact, why don't you invite them over for dinner?" Mrs. Barton said. "I think we should all get to know each other."

Sam thought that was a great idea.

"Sam was so surprised when he saw David!" Elizabeth exclaimed.

"*He* was surprised?" Jessica replied. "I thought *I* was going to die."

"Well, it would have been a convenient place to do it." Elizabeth smiled. "Right near the graveyard!"

Elizabeth, Jessica, and their brother Steven were eating pizza in the family room. Mr. and Mrs. Wakefield were out at a dinner party. Steven was trying to watch TV, but the twins were too excited about Sam and David to keep quiet.

"You guys," Steven complained, "I can't concentrate on the TV with all this noise."

"Are you telling us that you need absolute silence to understand a game show?" Elizabeth said mischieviously.

Jessica laughed.

"You'll be sorry for that comment," Steven said in a deep, threatening voice.

Jessica laughed harder. "Hey," she said to Elizabeth a moment later, "what if we were like Sam and David and you had never seen me before today?" She flashed a winning smile at her sister. "What kind of person would you think I was?"

Elizabeth couldn't resist. "A person with a messy room who never picks up her clothes."

"I should have left you in the cemetery," Jessica said in a disgusted tone of voice. "Maybe the ghosts would have gotten you."

"Ghosts?" Steven said turning to Jessica. "Do you really believe in ghosts?"

Jessica tried to pretend she hadn't heard him. She didn't want him to know how much he had scared her with his story about the graveyard.

Steven shook his head and laughed. "Sometimes you guys act like a couple of sixth graders," he said.

"But we *are* sixth—" Jessica started to protest, but stopped suddenly when she realized Steven was joking.

Steven got up and went to the kitchen to refill his milk glass, but the twins could hear him laughing.

"Do you think we can trade him, Lizzie?"

"Trade him? For what?" Elizabeth asked.

"A *nice* older brother who brings cute friends home."

Just then the television and all of the lights in the house went off!

"Very funny! Oldest trick in the book, Steven!" Elizabeth shouted.

They heard Steven scream. Next came the sound of something bouncing and rolling down the basement stairs. Then there was silence.

"Lizzie!" Jessica whispered. She grabbed Elizabeth's arm quickly. Elizabeth jumped.

"It's not funny, Steven," Elizabeth called.

There was no answer, and for a moment Elizabeth wondered if something really had happened to her brother.

Just then Elizabeth and Jessica heard a low moaning. It sounded like someone who was half-alive and half-dead.

"Elizabeth, what is that?"

"It's probably Steven trying to scare us."

"No, it's not," Jessica said with a trembling voice.

The moaning started again. First it sounded as if it was coming from the kitchen. Then they heard it from the dining room, and then from the hallway. As it got nearer it changed to a deep, evil laugh.

"It's a ghost!" Jessica cried. "It's coming closer, Lizzie. Let's get out of here." Jessica started pulling on her sister's arm.

"Rrroooowl," the hideous voice roared, suddenly closeby.

"It's in the room, Lizzie!" Jessica shrieked. Elizabeth and Jessica ran out of the family room, bumping into things and trying to find the basement stairs. There was a flashlight attached to the stairway wall with a magnet, and Elizabeth grabbed it on her way down. She and Jessica could still hear the horrible noise in the rooms above them.

Elizabeth went straight to the circuit breaker box and found the master power switch turned off. She flipped it on and the lights came back on.

"Very funny," Jessica said without smiling.

They went upstairs and back into the family room. The lights and the television were on, but there was no sign of Steven.

Suddenly Jessica gasped. "Look!" she said, pointing at the coffee table. "It's gone. *All* the pizza is gone. Steven took it all!"

"He even took the pieces *we* were eating!" Elizabeth said.

Then they heard the awful laughter again—but this time it was coming from Steven's bedroom.

"Let's get out of here," Sam whispered to David.

David nodded. The two of them quietly crept out of the Bartons' living room and headed for the stairs.

When Sam had called his parents earlier, they had immediately agreed to come over and meet the Bartons. The boys' parents got along instantly. First they told stories about David and Sam. Then Mrs. Barton brought out scrapbooks full of David's baby pictures. After a couple of hours, Sam was more than ready to escape from the living room.

"I'll show you where my room is," David said, taking the steps two at a time.

"I don't believe it," Sam exclaimed when they walked into David's room. "You have your baseball cards displayed on your bulletin board just like I do! Nobody else I know does that!"

"I didn't see any baseball cards when we were at your house," David said.

"That's because I haven't put my bulletin board up yet! We just moved in, remember? And look at this," Sam said, walking over to David's bookshelf. "You have so many of the same books that I have. This is incredible."

David smiled. "Well, what did you expect? We're twins."

"Yeah. I guess we really are. OK, what's your favorite movie?" Sam asked with an expectant look on his face.

"*Galaxy of Doom*," David answered.

"Mine, too," Sam said, beaming.

"I just thought of something," David said quietly, with a faraway look in his eyes. "You know the last scene in the movie, when they come back from outer space and meet their families in San Francisco? Every time I see that, I feel like I've been there, even though I've never been to San Francisco."

"That's just how I've felt ever since we came to Sweet Valley," Sam exclaimed. "You probably felt that way because of me—because I was there.

"Hey, I just got a great idea," he said after a pause. "Our birthdays are coming up next week, right? Let's have a double birthday party!"

"Cool!" David said. The boys ran downstairs to ask their parents. They decided to put the celebration off for a day or two in order to have more time to plan a big party.

Later, David pulled out the trundle bed from under his own bed. Both boys crawled under their sheets.

"I was just thinking . . ." Sam started. His voice trailed off.

"What?"

"About something I've never told anyone before," Sam said. "About a dream I have all the time."

David quickly sat up in his bed and looked over at Sam. "What dream?" he asked. He sounded very serious.

Sam's eyes caught David's for a minute and

they stared at each other. David seemed to know what Sam was going to say.

"There's an old man—" Sam began.

"—and he's walking in a thunderstorm," David finished for him. "I've had the same dream."

Sam didn't say anything for a minute. He felt a little scared.

"Have you ever seen the old man's face?" Sam asked.

"Only a little. It's raining too hard to see much," David said. "The wind is stronger than he is. He keeps trying to walk but the wind keeps blowing him back."

"But he never gives up," Sam said. "And I never get to the end of the dream. I mean, nothing ever happens."

"I know," David said. "That's the awful part. It never ends."

"Where do you think he's going?" Sam asked his twin.

David just shook his head.

Sam was quiet for a minute, reliving the dream in his head.

"Sam?"

"What?"

"I hope we don't dream about the old man again tonight."

"Me, too."

*   *   *

Sam could see himself when the lightning flashed. Or was it David? He couldn't tell. It was raining too hard. The thunder was deafening. Then he saw the old man again. He had to see the man's face! But even though the man was walking toward Sam, he never got any closer.

With a gasp, Sam woke up. David sat up, too, blinking in the morning sun. "I had the dream," Sam said.

David nodded. "But it was longer this time. It went on *forever*," he added. "What do you think it means?"

"I don't know," Sam said, hugging his knees. "I feel like the old man in the dream is trying to send us a message."

The two boys were quiet for a moment. Then Sam asked, "Do you have any pictures of our natural parents?"

David hopped out of bed and reached into a drawer in his dresser. From underneath a pile of socks, he pulled out a small framed photograph and handed it to Sam.

"This isn't anything like the picture I have," Sam said, staring at the photo. "And look! I don't believe it! They're standing in front of that house!"

"It's just an old house," David said. "It's not important."

"It's important to *me*," Sam said. "I've been riding past it on my bike ever since I came to

Sweet Valley. Something draws me there—I just can't stay away. It's really creepy."

"You *could* stay away from it if you really wanted to. You must want to go," David said.

"No, it's not like that," Sam said, shaking his head. "I feel like I don't have any choice." He explained how he had investigated the house with Elizabeth and Jessica, and had found out it used to belong to Jeremiah Seever.

David shrugged. "I guess I'm not too interested in the past," he said. "Or dead people."

Sam nodded slowly. He was beginning to notice that he and his twin were not *exactly* alike. Sam wanted to know everything he could about his natural parents, and the rest of the Burroughs family. But David didn't care. It made Sam a little sad. He had thought that if anyone would understand the way he felt, David would.

Sam studied the photograph, looking for a clue. His father looked happy. Sam could tell he was smiling under his bushy mustache. His mom looked pretty, and was laughing. Then Sam looked at the old house in the background and noticed a face in the upstairs window. It looked like an old man, but it was impossible to make out the person's features.

"Look," Sam said to David, pointing at the face. "Who is that?"

"I don't know. Why?"

"Because I went to the house the other day,

and I thought I saw someone standing in that window," Sam told him excitedly, pointing to the window in the picture.

"Maybe the house isn't really empty," David said. "Wouldn't it be cool if someone is secretly living there? Or maybe it's haunted!"

"I wonder why our parents had their picture taken there," Sam said.

"Yeah, I wonder," David said. But he didn't sound all that interested.

Just then David's father knocked on the bedroom door. "Time to get moving, David," he said, poking his head in the door. "Today's the day you and I are supposed to go shopping for a new bike, remember? An early birthday present," he explained to Sam.

"Great!" David said. "Can Sam come along?"

"If he wants to," Mr. Barton replied.

"I don't know," Sam said, hesitating. "I was thinking of looking at that house."

"Come with me to the bike shop, and then after lunch I'll go with you to the house," David suggested.

"Great!" Sam said. He started to smile, but then he got a strange look on his face.

"What's wrong?" David asked.

"Nothing," Sam said. "I'm just wondering what we'll find there."

Eleven

◇

Lila called Jessica after breakfast. "I was just thinking," Lila said in a serious voice.

"What?" Jessica was trying to wriggle into her sweater and talk on the phone at the same time.

"Well, it seems so weird. You know, about you being Lillian Barnes. It sort of gives me the creeps."

Jessica bit her lip. Her friend sounded a little scared. "It's not so bad," she said. "It's not like it changes my life or anything."

"But you were murdered in your past life!" Lila reminded her. "What if the same things happen to you in all your lives, Jessica? What if you—"

"Don't be silly," Jessica said quickly. "Nothing like that is going to happen to me."

There was a pause. "You never know," Lila said.

Jessica made a face. She was suddenly sorry about teasing her friend. She remembered how scared she was the night before, when Steven had tricked her with the lights and the moaning. Her friend was really worried! "Listen, Lila—" she began.

"So I think you should try to remember where the gold is, Jessica," Lila went on. "Really soon, too. Just in case."

Jessica raised her eyebrows. Maybe Lila wasn't worried about her after all! Maybe Lila just cared about finding the gold! Suddenly Jessica didn't feel bad at all about teasing her. "I'll try," she promised. "I'll do my best."

"My father can tell you what to do with it when you find it," Lila went on. She was beginning to sound like her old know-it-all self again. "He knows all about taking care of money."

"OK, Lila," Jessica agreed. She stuck her tongue out at the phone. "I'm going to the record store with Elizabeth today. But let's talk about it some more when I get home, all right?"

"Sure. I'll call you later." Lila hung up.

Jessica hung up the phone and snapped her fingers. "I'm going to teach you a lesson, Lila Fowler!"

"Favorite food?" David asked in the car on the way to the bike shop.

"Spaghetti with clam sauce," Sam answered.

"All right!" David yelled. "Me, too. Anything with clams, actually. How about your favorite sport?"

"Well, I love to juggle," Sam said. "But my favorite team sport is soccer."

"Soccer is mine, too," David told him. "But I don't know how to juggle. Hey, if you'll teach me to juggle I'll teach you some magic tricks."

"Great," Sam said with a smile. It was terrific having a brother. And driving around Sweet Valley with David and his dad made Sam feel like he instantly fit in. *Maybe Sweet Valley isn't so bad after all,* Sam thought.

Then Sam realized they were heading toward the marina because the bike shop was located on a street across from the piers. His heart sank. He closed his eyes but he could still see the seascape in front of him. There was something powerful in his memory about this place. *I must have been here before,* he thought.

"What's wrong?" David asked, noticing the look on Sam's face.

"I don't know," Sam answered. "It's just that every time I come here, it's kind of like being at that old house. I feel like I've been here before." Sam paused for a moment. He had an idea. "Mr. Barton, is this where my natural parents had their accident?" he asked.

"No, Sam, I don't think it is," Mr. Barton

said quietly. He pulled the car into a space and turned off the ignition.

"Let's go," Sam said, jumping out of the car. He wanted to get the errand done and get away from the marina as quickly as possible.

As they were crossing the parking lot, Sam heard a familiar voice call his name. He turned around and saw Elizabeth waving to him from across the street. "You go on," Sam said to David and Mr. Barton. "I'm going to talk to Elizabeth for a minute."

Elizabeth crossed the street quickly. Jessica was only a few steps behind her.

"Hi!" Elizabeth said. "How's it going with your new twin brother?"

"Great," Sam replied. "He's in the bike shop picking out a new off-road bike for his birthday."

"Off-road bike? Wow!" Jessica said. "That's a terrific present."

"Yeah," Sam agreed. "David's dad is really great. After David picks it out I've got to go home for lunch, but right after that we're going to the old mansion." Sam explained about the photograph David had of the house.

"I'll bet there *is* someone living there," Jessica said, lowering her voice. She leaned toward Sam. "You have to call us the minute you get home and tell us exactly what you find out!"

"Why don't you guys meet us there?" Sam asked. "Around three o'clock?"

By this time, Elizabeth and Jessica felt like they were part of the mystery as well. They both agreed to come.

Sam got home just in time for lunch. His mother was making tuna salad in the kitchen.

"Hi, Mom," Sam said, opening the refrigerator. He pulled out the milk and began to pour himself a glass. Then he noticed that his mother wasn't speaking.

"Mom?" he asked.

Mrs. Sloane turned around. Her eyes were red.

"What's wrong, Mom?" Sam asked in a concerned voice.

"Oh, it's just—" Mrs. Sloane clasped her hands together. "I don't want to lose you," she said.

"Lose me?" Sam frowned. "What are you talking about?"

His mother held out her hands. "Now that you've found David—"

It took Sam a few moments to understand what she meant. "Mom, just because I've found David it doesn't mean that I love you and Dad any less."

His mother smiled. "That's good. Because no matter what, you know we love you very much."

Sam looked at his mother. No matter what

crazy things were happening to him, she would always be there for him. He went to her and hugged her tight.

"It's OK, Mom," he said. He felt embarrassed, but he was glad, too.

She hugged him back.

When Sam and David got to the mansion later that afternoon, Jessica and Elizabeth were already there.

"The gate's unlocked," Jessica told them. She sounded excited and nervous at the same time. "Let's go in."

They opened the creaky iron gate and walked through the front yard of the strange old house. The stone path they walked along was overgrown with weeds.

"Listen!" David said. "I hear something."

It sounded like digging, but it was faint.

"I think it's coming from the backyard," Elizabeth said.

They walked slowly toward the back of the house. When they turned the corner, they saw an elderly man hoeing a patch of the garden. He wore baggy blue jeans and a plaid work shirt, and a large straw hat covered his thick white hair.

"Hi," Jessica called to him.

The man looked up and watched them come closer. He didn't seem surprised that they were there. In fact, he looked as if he had been expecting them.

Sam felt his heart skip a beat. "David," Sam whispered to his brother, "it's—it's the man in our dream!"

"Don't be crazy," David said, but he sounded frightened. "You said yourself that you couldn't see his face in the dream."

"I don't care," Sam said softly. "There's something familiar about him. I've seen him before, I know it."

"Do you think he lives here?" David asked.

"Maybe," Sam said. He felt a sudden chill. He looked at David and knew instantly that David was feeling it, too. Elizabeth and Jessica seemed unaware of anything out of the ordinary.

Elizabeth gave the old man a big smile. "Hello," she said cheerfully.

"Hello," the man replied. He stretched, and then leaned on his hoe as if it were a walking stick. He gazed steadily at his visitors. He seemed to stare hardest at Sam and David, who were hanging back. "It's not every day that one gets an opportunity to look at four people and see only two faces," the man said.

Elizabeth and Jessica laughed and introduced themselves. Elizabeth looked at Sam, but he kept quiet.

"I'm pleased to make your acquaintances,"

said the man, making a small, formal bow. "I'm the caretaker."

Jessica looked around at the unmowed grass, the huge weeds, and the run-down house. "It doesn't look like anyone's taking care of this place," she mumbled.

"Jessica," Elizabeth said reproachfully.

The caretaker tilted his head back and laughed. "You say what you think, don't you, young lady?" he remarked to Jessica. "That's an admirable quality."

Who is this man? Sam wondered. He had such a formal way of talking, not like his parents or even his teachers.

"We haven't seen you here before," Elizabeth said.

"Some things don't always need tending to," the caretaker said. "I come when they do." His piercing eyes gazed at Sam and David again. Then he pushed back his large straw hat so he could wipe his forehead with the sleeve of his plaid work shirt. "So, you've been here before, have you? Would you like to see my garden?"

"I love flowers," Elizabeth said enthusiastically.

Slowly, the caretaker led the way through the twists and turns of the large flower garden. All kinds of flowers were in bloom. But the shrubs and paths around the garden were uncared for.

"There used to be annuals here, but not anymore," the caretaker said. "Now all that's left are the perennials. Do you know what I'm talking about?"

"Well," Elizabeth said, "I know that annuals live only one season. You plant them, they bloom, and then they die. But perennial flowers grow back year after year, don't they?"

"Yes. And I am fondest of the perennials," the caretaker said. "I marvel at the miracle of their coming back to life. It's like having a second chance."

A second chance for what? Sam wondered. He grabbed David's arm to keep him back.

"There's something strange about this guy, don't you think?" Sam whispered.

David looked nervous. He cleared his throat and took a deep breath. "I think you're just getting spooked. He's just an ordinary old guy, nothing else," he said.

"Then what's he doing here?" Sam wondered out loud.

"Taking care of the place," David said, but he didn't really sound convinced.

"Ask him his name," Sam whispered to his twin.

"OK," David said. When they caught up to the caretaker, Sam saw that the man had picked some flowers and given them to Jessica and Elizabeth.

"Excuse me," David said, "but what did you say your name was?"

"Oh, so you boys *can* talk when you want to," said the old man with a laugh. "That's good news. I'm P.J. And who, may I ask, are you?"

"I'm David, and this is my brother, Sam."

"I'm extremely pleased to meet you," the caretaker said.

Sam looked back at the eerie old mansion. "Have you worked here a long time?" he asked.

"What may seem like a long time to you seems a very short time to me," P.J. said with a smile.

"Did you ever know our parents?" Sam asked. "Their names were Ted and Julie Burroughs. They had their picture taken in front of this house once." Sam nudged his brother, who reached into a pocket and took out a photograph of their parents. He showed it to the old man.

P.J. looked at the photo for a long time before handing it back to David.

"The Burroughses used to own this house," the caretaker said slowly.

I knew it, I knew it, I knew it, Sam thought. The words pounded over and over again in his head. Now all the feelings he'd had about the house made sense! Sam wanted to ask the man a million questions, and at the same time he was afraid. For a moment he couldn't speak.

"I *knew* this house had something to do with us," he finally said. "But why did the woman next door say that some old rich guy—Jeremiah Seever—owned the house?"

"This house did belong to Jeremiah Seever, Sam. But before that, it was owned by the Burroughs family."

"Why did they sell it?" Sam asked, disappointed.

"They didn't. It's a sad story, Sam. Are you certain you want to hear it?" P.J. asked.

Sam nodded.

"And you, David?"

"Uh, sure," David said with a shrug.

P.J. began his story. "The house was built by the Burroughs family and passed down for many generations. The last Burroughs to own it was Peter Burroughs."

That was a name Sam recognized.

"That unfortunate man," P.J. said, "had he lived, would have had the great fortune to know you, his great-grandsons." The caretaker paused for a moment. "But something tragic happened," he said.

"What?" Sam asked, his heart pounding in his chest.

"Well, for almost their entire lives Peter Burroughs and Jeremiah Seever were the best of friends. They were boys together and they grew into young men together. Everyone said they were like brothers. Boys, your great-grandfather was a dreamer, an inventor. He didn't care about money."

"I'll bet Jeremiah did," Jessica said. "The woman next door said he was really cheap."

"Yes," P.J. said. "Jeremiah was always clever about money. Well, one day these two best friends decided to start a business together. They were going to build a factory. But they needed a lot of money to build it." P.J. looked far off into the distance, as if he were trying to capture a memory.

"Did they get the money?" Jessica asked impatiently.

"Yes, they did. To raise the money, Peter Burroughs mortgaged this house, his family's house. That way he was able to borrow enough money to start the business. And the business became a great success."

P.J. reached out and picked a few flowers before continuing.

"I wish the story ended there," P.J. said. "But it doesn't." He paused, then turned to Sam with a questioning look. "What would you do if you thought your best friend was trying to cheat you?" the caretaker asked.

"Well, I'm not sure," Sam said. "I guess he wouldn't be my friend anymore."

"Was Jeremiah cheating Peter?" Jessica asked.

"Peter thought so," the caretaker answered. "And Jeremiah thought he was being cheated by Peter. They argued. It was a terrible argument, and after that they dissolved their partnership, sold their business, and never spoke a single word to each other again."

"In their *entire* lives?" Jessica asked. She took pride in the fact that no one could stay angry at her for more than a day.

"In their entire lives," P.J. confirmed. "Twelve months later, Peter Burroughs was dead."

"I don't get it," said David. "If this was the Burroughs' house, then how did Jeremiah Seever get it?"

"Through cheating and lying," P.J. said. His face was calm, but there was anger in his voice. "After your great-grandfather's death, Jeremiah produced legal papers that he said proved the house belonged to him. According to the papers, Peter had given the house to Jeremiah as part of the agreement when they sold their business."

"And it wasn't true?" asked David.

The caretaker shook his head. "But the court believed Jeremiah. So Peter's widow and his children were forced to move out of the house. Jeremiah Seever moved in, and spent the remaining years of his sad, lonely, and miserable life here."

"Hey, you guys," Jessica said to David and Sam. "That means this house should have been yours."

Sam looked at the house longingly as if getting it back could somehow also bring back all of his dead relatives. "Who was Michael Burroughs?" he asked the caretaker after a pause. "I saw his grave. He was really young when he died."

A sudden change came over P.J.'s face. "I can't stand here telling stories all day," he said. "I've got work to do." His voice sounded angry.

"But did Michael live here, too? How did he die?" Sam asked.

Without another word, P.J. turned his back on them and walked quickly toward the house.

Sam ran to catch up with the caretaker, who was just walking around the side of the mansion. "P.J.!" Sam called. But when Sam turned the corner, he couldn't believe his eyes. The caretaker was gone. He had vanished into thin air!

Twelve

◇

On Sunday, Jessica woke up feeling worried. What had happened to P.J.? The old mansion was a pretty creepy place, she decided. But it was also the perfect place for the practical joke she was going to play on Lila. She decided not to think about P.J. anymore.

The more Jessica thought about her trick, the more cheerful she became. She giggled when she remembered how serious Lila was about the hidden gold. Jessica lay on her back and planned what to do next. Lila was already hooked. It was time to give the trick its finishing touch.

With a mischievous grin, Jessica got up, went to her closet, and started hunting through the piles of things on the floor. Somewhere she had a small wooden box.

When she finally found it underneath a pair of sandals that didn't fit anymore, she took it to her desk. Then she wrote "Fooled you, Lila!" on a piece of paper, folded it up, and put it in the box. Now all she had to do was hide the box somewhere at the old mansion, and take Lila there to look for it. It was the perfect end to the joke.

"Where are you going?" Elizabeth was standing in the bathroom doorway.

Jessica tied her sneakers carefully and didn't look at her sister. "Umm . . . I have to do something with Lila," she said. She was pretty sure Elizabeth wouldn't like her plan. Elizabeth hated to do anything mean to anyone, and she would never understand why Jessica was making the joke last so long.

"See you later," Jessica said. She grabbed the box and ran out of her room.

A while later, Jessica turned her bike down McClarendon Street. The old house was just as spooky-looking as ever.

What if it really is haunted? she wondered as she leaned her bike against the fence. The gate made a loud *screeeek* when she opened it.

"There's no such thing as ghosts," Jessica said out loud. Her footsteps sounded very loud on the stone path, and she felt as though the overgrown weeds were reaching out to grab her legs.

Jessica realized she was holding her breath. She let it out slowly, and then made herself look up at the windows. They looked back down at her like blank eyes.

She was almost positive that someone was watching her! Could it be P.J.? There was no sign of him.

"There's no such thing as ghosts," she repeated to herself. A breeze rustled the ivy on the house. It made a whispering sound that scared Jessica. Quickly, she ran around to the backyard with the box held tightly in her hand.

A tall pine tree stood by the rusty iron fence. Underneath it was a wide area covered with old, dry pine needles. It was the only place in the yard that wasn't full of weeds. Jessica kneeled down, brushed away a layer of needles, and put her box in the shallow hole. Then she covered it up again.

Suddenly Jessica got that prickly feeling again. Someone *was* watching her, she was sure! Wincing, she turned around and looked at the house.

"P.J.?" she called in a shaky voice.

There was no answer. The old caretaker wasn't around. Jessica was surrounded by emptiness and silence. The straggly weeds waved back and forth in the breeze.

Jessica couldn't stay there a minute longer. She ran back out to the gate, jumped on her bike, and pedaled home to safety as fast as she could!

Elizabeth watched the egg roll toward the end of the counter. It wobbled dangerously on to the edge, but there was nothing she could do to stop it—her hands were already full. She closed her eyes and hoped the egg would stop by itself.

Crack! Elizabeth felt something gooey hit her ankle. She opened one eye and saw the egg splattered all over her sneakers. She sighed loudly.

It was Monday and Elizabeth was back in the kitchen, fixing another dinner—by herself. She had given up any hope of Jessica showing up in time to do her share of the work.

A minute later, Steven walked into the kitchen and went directly to the refrigerator. He grabbed two apples and was about to leave when he noticed Elizabeth's sneakers. "Usually people *eat* eggs," he commented to his sister, "they don't wear them."

Elizabeth tried to stay calm. "Accidents happen. No one's perfect."

"No one's perfect? Then how do you explain me?" said Steven, his mouth full of apple.

"I can't explain you," Elizabeth said grumpily. "I'm waiting for modern science to do that."

Steven laughed as he strolled out of the room.

Elizabeth carefully put down everything she was carrying, cleaned up the mess, and went back to making cream puffs for dessert.

Mr. Wakefield peeked into the kitchen. "Everything smells great," he said encouragingly.

Elizabeth knew he was checking on her because he was hungry. "Everything's going to be late, Dad," she said. "It's taking me a long time to do everything by myself."

"No rush," he said. He smiled as he left.

Finally Jessica breezed in the back door. "Hi, Lizzie," she said. "I hope dinner isn't going to be late. I've got some really important plans—"

"Jessica!" Elizabeth interruped her twin. "The spaghetti sauce bubbled out all over the stove, I cut myself slicing the garlic bread, and I dropped an egg on my foot making cream puffs. *Where have you been?*"

"Boy, you're having a bad day, Elizabeth," Jessica answered innocently.

"Jess, you said you'd be here to help. It's Monday, remember?"

"It's not my fault, Lizzie." Jessica explained. "Janet Howell said we had to stay at the mall until Mr. Bowman showed up. We heard he was going clothes shopping today, and we just *had* to be there to see him pick out his ties. You know how awfully he dresses. Anyway, he didn't show up, but Janet just wouldn't let us leave.''

Jessica smiled and Elizabeth wondered whether that meant she was telling the truth or she was pleased with the story she had thought up.

''Well, at least you can help me now,'' Elizabeth said.

''I can't. I'm really sorry, but some of the Unicorns are sleeping over at Lila's house tonight. We just decided on our way home from the mall. Isn't this the most fabulous vacation ever?''

''Jess, I'm making all of *your* favorite foods!'' Elizabeth moaned.

''That is *so* nice.'' Jessica gave Elizabeth one of her sweetest smiles. ''And I'd love to stay. But Lila wants me there early to help her make tacos.''

''You're cooking at *Lila's* house?'' Elizabeth couldn't believe her ears. ''Did you ask Mom and Dad yet?''

''Good idea,'' Jessica said, heading toward the living room.

''Jess, what about *this* dinner?''

''Save me some, OK? Thanks.'' Jessica dashed out of the kitchen.

I'll do better than that, Elizabeth thought to herself. *Don't you worry, Jessica Wakefield.*

* * *

The Unicorns had their sleeping bags arranged on the floor in Lila's gigantic bedroom. Janet and Ellen were braiding Tamara's hair in dozens of tiny braids. Lila was playing a Johnny Buck album on her stereo and painting her fingernails different colors.

Jessica went to the bathroom door. She waited until she caught Lila's eye and beckoned with her finger. "Come here," Jessica mouthed.

Lila pointed at herself and raised her eyebrows. When Jessica nodded, Lila quickly put down the pink nail polish she was using and hurried over. They shut the bathroom door.

"I had to tell you," Jessica began seriously. "I had this dream last night. It was so weird!"

"About being Lillian Barnes?" Lila whispered. Her eyes opened wide.

Jessica nodded. "Remember that house we went to? I think it *is* the right place."

"Wow!" Lila gasped. "Are you sure the gold is there?"

"I don't know." Jessica shrugged. "I kept seeing this tree, a big tall tree."

Lila frowned. "Who cares about a stupid tree! Where's the gold?"

"I don't know. All I remember is that I was looking for it, and I kept seeing this tree," Jessica said.

Suddenly Lila let out a gasp. "I know—it's under the tree! I bet that's it, Jessica."

"Do you want to go look?" Jessica asked. "I mean, it's pretty creepy there."

"Who cares!" Lila said. "I have to go to the dentist tomorrow afternoon. But I think I'll be home by four-thirty."

"Hey!" Janet knocked on the bathroom door. "What are you guys talking about?"

Lila grabbed Jessica's arm and put one finger over her lips. "Nothing!" she called out. She looked at Jessica and shook her head.

"We want to tell fortunes," Janet said through the door. "Hurry up."

"We're coming," Lila said. She turned to Jessica and lowered her voice. "Let's do it tomorrow after I get back from the dentist."

Jessica picked up Lila's hairbrush and started brushing her hair. She looked at herself in the mirror, and tried not to smile. "OK," she said in a serious voice. "Let's meet at the house on McClarendon Street at five o'clock."

"It's a deal," Lila said.

Part of Jessica wanted to forget the whole thing. Just thinking about going back to the old house gave her the creeps. Maybe it was true that mean people left bad vibrations in a house. Maybe Jeremiah Seever was still there in spirit, and that was why the house made Jessica so uncomfortable!

But another part of Jessica couldn't wait to see Lila's face when she found the note. It was too good to miss! Jessica put down the hairbrush and nodded.

"I can't wait to see what we find," Lila went on.

"Me neither," Jessica giggled. "I bet it'll be a big surprise!"

Today I'm going to find out more about my relatives, Sam decided on Tuesday morning. Ever since he had met the old caretaker at the Seever house, Sam had been more curious than ever to find out about his real family. But he had been so busy for the last few days getting to know David, he hadn't had time to do any investigating.

The trouble was, Sam had no idea how to find out what he wanted to know. He decided to call Elizabeth for advice.

She answered the phone on the first ring. "Hello?"

"Hi. It's Sam."

"Oh, hi! What's up?"

"I was wondering if you could help me." Sam explained his problem.

"I had to make a family tree for school last year," Elizabeth told him. "At City Hall they have birth and death records. It's a good place to start."

"I'm not too good at research," Sam told her. "But I'm going to try."

"Want some help?" Elizabeth offered.

"I think I *need* it," Sam replied.

Later that afternoon Sam and Elizabeth walked into the Clerk of Courts office at City Hall. It was a large room with a long, dark wooden counter. The office was old and its plaster walls had many coats of paint. The walls were bright yellow, but the room was still dim because it had only one small window. The one clerk on duty looked up when Sam and Elizabeth came in.

"What can I do for you?" the clerk asked, drumming his hands lightly on the counter top.

"I need some information about my relatives," Sam said.

"Well, you've come to the right place. Just fill out these forms, please."

Elizabeth helped Sam fill out the forms, and a few minutes later the clerk brought several thick, dusty books over to them.

"What are you doing?" the clerk asked. "Making your family tree?"

"Well, I—" Sam began awkwardly.

"Sam! I found one," Elizabeth interrupted him. "Here's Michael Burroughs," she said, pointing to a page in one of the books.

Sam read the entry slowly and then reread it because he couldn't believe his eyes. It was no mistake, but it was almost too amazing to be true.

Michael Burroughs had been born on the same day as Sam and his brother David. The year was different, but the day was *exactly* the same.

But the part that was really strange was Michael's date of death. Michael Burroughs had died exactly one day before his twelfth birthday. And tomorrow was the day before Sam and David's twelfth birthday!

"I can't read something here," Sam said to Elizabeth. "Can you make this out?"

She shook her head. The type was smudged.

Sam went over to the clerk to ask for help. Elizabeth followed him.

Sam pointed to the line that read "Cause of Death." "Can you read that?" Sam asked.

"No, I can't," the clerk replied. "Many of these old records are too faded to read."

"Well, what do you do when you can't read them?" Sam asked.

"Usually? Nothing."

"What about when it's really important?" Sam insisted.

"Is *this* really important?" the clerk asked with a faint smile.

Sam nodded.

"Well, if you're really interested, go check

out the old newspapers in the library. You know the date. Maybe there'll be a story about the boy's death."

"Great idea," Elizabeth said. "Come on, Sam, I'll help you."

"Thanks," Sam called to the clerk.

"Don't mention it."

Sam and Elizabeth hopped on their bikes and raced all the way to the Sweet Valley library. Sam couldn't wait to find the newspaper story. He felt like he was finally getting closer to knowing his real family.

They got to the library at exactly 5:01.

"I'm sorry, but the library is closed," the young librarian standing at the door said.

"I've got to look up something in an old newspaper," Sam told her. "It's very important."

"Sorry, the library's closed. You'll have to come back tomorrow. We open at ten."

"But I've *got* to see those newspapers," Sam pleaded as people filed past them on their way out.

"It's really important to him," Elizabeth chimed in. "We're trying to find out—"

"I really am sorry. We close at five. I can't let anyone in now." The librarian pointed to the large clock on the wall. It said 5:03. "Come back tomorrow."

"But tomorrow may be too late," Sam said. Deep inside he had the feeling that *something* was going to happen. He gave the librarian a desperate look.

"Come back tomorrow," she said firmly. She stepped inside the library doors and locked them behind her.

"It's not so bad, Sam," Elizabeth told him. "You can come back first thing in the morning."

"*I* can come back?" Sam asked. "Can't you come with me?" Sam couldn't explain it, but for some reason he didn't want to look at the newspapers by himself.

"I'm sorry," Elizabeth replied. "I have to babysit first thing tomorrow morning. I could meet you around eleven-thirty, but probably not before."

"Thanks," Sam said with a sigh, "but I don't want to wait—I guess I'll have to come alone."

Thirteen

◇

Jessica reached the old mansion first.

"Hi, Jessica!" Lila's voice called down the street.

Jessica watched her friend pull up on her bike. She almost decided to tell Lila the truth, but then she changed her mind. "Come on," she said, pushing open the creaky iron gate.

"This place is so spooky," Lila said in a hushed voice. "It looks like a prison or something with this huge fence all around."

Jessica shivered as she looked around. "I know."

"Where do we go?" Lila asked eagerly.

"Look for a big tall tree," Jessica said. She wanted to get the joke over with quickly. "Like a pine tree, maybe."

Lila peered around the overgrown yard. "Let's look in the back."

They went single file down the brambly path and around the corner of the house.

"Is this really the right place?" Lila asked. She sounded nervous. "Do you remember it from your past life?"

Jessica nodded, and then pointed to the pine tree. "There it is," she hissed.

"Wow!" Lila ran ahead, stopping under the towering tree. "Is the gold buried here?" When Jessica nodded, Lila found a stick and began poking it into the soft pine needles. "We should have brought a shovel or something," Lila complained.

Jessica stood back, waiting for her friend to find the little wooden box. She tried not to smile while she watched. Lila was going to be so surprised!

Finally, Lila's stick hit something. "Hey!" Lila cried. "Come here!" She began scraping away the pine needles. "Look!"

Jessica had to put both hands over her mouth to keep from laughing. Lila pulled out the old box and opened the lid. Her mouth dropped open when she saw the note.

"I got you!" Jessica burst out. She collapsed into giggles. "You really fell for it, Lila!" she managed to say. "I really had you fooled."

Lila closed the lid with a snap. Her face was

beet red and all she could do was glare at her friend. Jessica laughed even harder and leaned against the tree.

"This is the stupidest thing you've ever done, Jessica Wakefield!" Lila said in a quavery voice.

Jessica stopped laughing and wiped her eyes. "It's just a joke, Lila. Come on."

"Yeah, well, ha ha," Lila shot back angrily. "Here's what I think of your joke!"

She threw the wooden box to the ground and stalked off. Jessica heard the iron gate shut with a clang.

"You don't have to get so mad," Jessica grumbled. She bent over to pick up the box. Then she looked over her shoulder quickly. Were those footsteps she heard?

"Lila?" she called.

There was no answer. The ivy rustled on the side of the house.

"Lila?" Jessica called again. She had that strange feeling again, as though someone were watching her. Her mouth felt dry all of a sudden, and she looked around. It was getting dark. Jessica's heart began to go *thud-thud-thud* in her ears.

"Lila, come on out! I'm sorry," Jessica said in a fearful voice. "You can quit trying to scare me! You got me back."

But there was still no answer. Then Jessica heard a loud *crack!*

She spun around with a gasp. A loose shutter swung in the breeze and banged against the house with another loud noise. The rustling ivy sounded more like whispering than ever. Jessica stared up at the black, broken windows.

Before she knew what she was doing, she was running back to the front gate. She raced through the tall weeds and dead grass as fast as she could. When she reached the gate she tugged on it with all her strength.

But it wouldn't budge. She was locked in!

Elizabeth was riding home from the library when a strange feeling came over her. She stopped her bike at an intersection and frowned. She felt nervous, and a prickly sensation went up and down her spine. Why did she feel like going in a different direction all of a sudden?

She didn't know, and she didn't care. The feeling was getting stronger all the time, and she knew she had to do something. Whatever the reason, she felt she had to ride to the other side of town as quickly as she could. With a shock, she realized she was heading for McClarendon Street. The feeling was getting stronger all the time. Somehow she knew that something was happening to Jessica!

"Help! Help!" came a frantic voice as Elizabeth turned down McClarendon Street.

"Jessica?" Elizabeth pedaled even faster. When she reached the Seever house, she saw her twin sister crying and tugging wildly at the gate. Elizabeth jumped off her bike while it was still rolling.

"Lizzie, let me out!" Jessica begged. "It's locked!" Her face was scratched and streaked with tears.

Elizabeth ran to the gate. The catch was difficult to move, but she snapped it open.

"It wasn't locked, Jess," Elizabeth said. "What happened?"

Still crying, Jessica ran out of the gate and shook her head. "I couldn't open it, Lizzie!" she sobbed. "I was so scared. I thought a ghost was coming after me. I thought it was going to get me!"

"I know," Elizabeth said. She hugged her sister tight. "I could feel it, too."

Jessica sniffled. "You could?"

Elizabeth nodded. "I'm glad we're twins."

"Me, too," Jessica agreed seriously.

"But what were you doing here?" Elizabeth asked after Jessica stopped crying and began to calm down.

Jessica wiped her eyes with the back of her hand. "It was really dumb," she said. "I was playing a joke on Lila, and now she's really mad at me."

"You mean that reincarnation story?" Elizabeth asked in a surprised tone. "You mean you kept it up this long? Did you scare her?"

Jessica shrugged miserably. "I don't think so. But *I* was scared! I was never so sorry about anything in my whole life. I should never have come back here."

"If you tell Lila you're sorry, maybe she won't be so mad at you," Elizabeth suggested. Jessica nodded. "But what scared you, anyway?" Elizabeth went on.

Jessica looked back at the house and gulped. "I don't know. There's something so eerie here, Lizzie. I really think this place is haunted."

Elizabeth's stomach did a flip-flop. "Oh, come on, Jessica. It couldn't be." But she couldn't help feeling a little bit frightened.

"I think it is," Jessica stated firmly. "And Sam and David better stay away. I think it could be dangerous—especially for them." Her eyes looked enormous.

Elizabeth tried to shake off the uneasy feeling that was nagging her. She couldn't help wondering about Sam and David. Could they really be in danger?

Fourteen

◇

When he woke up the next morning, Sam realized he had had the nightmare about the old man and the storm again. It had been stronger and clearer—and more frightening—than ever before. This time, Sam thought he had almost been able to see the old man's face. And there was something familiar about it. Was it P.J.? Sam wasn't sure.

What does the dream mean? Sam wondered for what seemed like the millionth time. Quickly he threw on some clothes and ran downstairs. It was after nine o'clock. The library would be opening soon, and Sam wanted to be there as early as possible.

"Where're you going in such a hurry?" Sam's

father called to him from where he sat reading on the front porch.

"Library," Sam said as he came out the door. He bent down to tie his sneaker.

"On a beautiful day like today? I'm surprised you don't want to be outside playing ball or something," his father said.

"I can't. I'm trying to find out about . . ." Sam stopped. He wondered if his mom and dad were hurt that he was so interested in his natural parents.

"Your natural parents? I know," Mr. Sloane said. "And I think that's great."

"Thanks, Dad." Sam grinned.

"Listen, I'm heading over to see a new job site soon, and your mother will be out all day, too. Are you OK for lunch and everything?"

"Yeah. Don't worry. See you later," Sam said. A few minutes later, he climbed on his bike and rode off.

Sam got to the library twenty minutes before it opened. The librarian was just arriving. She gave Sam a big smile and nodded. Sam felt relieved.

"Great day," the librarian said, taking a deep breath and looking around. "Almost a shame to go inside." She unlocked the door and Sam raced up the steps to go in with her. But she turned and blocked his way. "It's not ten yet," she said. "Wait outside, please." She closed the door behind her and locked it.

Sam sighed. Couldn't she see how anxious he was? He sat down heavily on the library steps. A peculiar feeling was starting to build up inside of him. Something was going to happen today—something bad.

Sam's thoughts wandered back to the nightmare, and then to David. He had tried to call David twice the day before to see if he would come to the library. Both times, nobody had answered the phone at the Bartons'. Sam had been a little disappointed, and now he felt more anxious than ever. For some reason he didn't understand, he needed to talk to David immediately. *I'll call him as soon as I get home*, Sam told himself.

When the library doors were finally unlocked, Sam rushed inside.

"I need some help!" Sam told the librarian. "It's urgent."

"What's the matter?" the librarian asked, clearly alarmed. "Are you hurt?"

"Hurt?" Sam echoed, surprised. "No, I'm fine. I need to see a newspaper from thirty years ago. Everything that happened around this date."

The librarian gave Sam a strange look, but she went into another room and came back with a spool of microfilm in a small box. She showed Sam how to load the microfilm into the viewing machine and then went back to the desk. Sam began to turn the crank, advancing the film. Day by day, page by page, the months surrounding Michael Burroughs's death whirled by Sam on the screen.

Finally Sam slowed down and then stopped. "This is it," he whispered. "This is really it."

The front page headline of the *Sweet Valley News* read, "Local Businessman and Grandson Drown in Boating Accident." The date on the paper was his birthday.

Sam's hands were clammy and he wiped them on his jeans. Then he began to read the article carefully.

Peter J. Burroughs, 59, and his grandson, Michael Burroughs, 11, drowned yesterday in a boating accident during a severe storm.

According to family members, Mr. Burroughs had taken his young grandson on a boating trip during fair weather to celebrate the boy's twelfth birthday, which would have been today.

Mr. Burroughs, who was an accomplished sailor, owned his own boat, the *Eclectic*.

There were several eyewitnesses who saw the accident from the shore. "The sky got dark all of a sudden," said Mr. Casey Dolan, of Sweet Valley. "It was the most ferocious squall I've ever seen. The water turned white in what seemed like a second. I saw the boat capsize and I saw Mr. Burroughs and the youngster go into the water. He was trying to save the boy, but the waves were too strong."

"It was awful," said Walter Wager, another witness. "The waves overpowered them. If anyone had gone out to try to save them, they would have been drowned themselves."

Until a year ago Mr. Burroughs was the co-owner of Useful Tools, a manufacturing business he began in Sweet Valley with his partner, Jeremiah Seever.

(Continued on page 23)

Sam turned the crank, and on page twenty-three he found a long article about Peter Burroughs. Then he noticed the two photographs at the top of the page. Sam couldn't believe what he was seeing.

One photograph was of Michael Burroughs. He looked very much like Sam and David. He almost had the same face, the same hair, and the same expression they did. The other photograph was of Peter Burroughs. Sam couldn't stop staring at it. The kind, steady eyes and the easy smile were unmistakable. Peter Burroughs looked *exactly* like P.J., the caretaker at Jeremiah Seever's mansion! But Peter Burroughs had died thirty years ago.

Sam suddenly jumped up and raced to the telephone. He *had* to talk to David.

"Hello, Sam," Mrs. Barton said when she answered the telephone. "I'm sorry, but David's not here."

"Where is he?" Sam asked. "I've really got to talk to him."

"His father took him sailing."

Sailing. The word echoed in Sam's mind. He felt numb.

"Hello, Sam? Are you still there?"

"He went sailing?" Sam said in a dull voice.

"It's such a beautiful day, so they decided to go at the last minute," David's mother said. "They tried to call you to see if you wanted to go along, too, but no one answered at your house. They left just a little while ago."

Sam hung up the phone. His hands were shaking. Now he was truly afraid something terrible was going to happen. Thirty years ago there had been a boating accident. A boy and a man had drowned in a sudden storm, one day before the boy's twelfth birthday. That boy had the same birthday as David and Sam. And tomorrow was their birthday. It was too odd to be a coincidence. Sam was convinced the same thing was going to happen to David and his father!

Sam ran out of the library and unchained his bike. He didn't know where to go or what to do, but he had to stop his brother from going out on that boat!

Sam took a deep breath and tried to clear his head. He had to think of the fastest way to get to the marina. It was a long way, through a busy section of town, and it would take Sam a long time to get there on his bike. His parents couldn't drive him because they had both gone shopping for the day. Then he thought of Elizabeth and Jessica. The Wakefields didn't live very far from the library. If he asked them, maybe Mr. or Mrs. Wakefield would give him a ride to the marina.

Sam jumped on his bike and raced to the Wakefields' house. He dropped his bike in the front yard and ran to the door. He rang the bell and banged on the door at the same time.

"Jessica," Sam gasped when she opened the door, "are your parents home? It's important!"

"No, just me and Elizabeth," Jessica said. "Why? What's wrong?"

"It's David," Sam said. "He's in danger!"

"What's going on?" Elizabeth said, appearing in the doorway behind Jessica. She looked frightened. "Sam, what's wrong?"

Sam pushed past them into the house. "You've got to listen to me. Even if you think I'm crazy, just help me, because if we don't hurry I'm sure David's going to die."

Quickly Sam told them about the newspaper article and the photographs.

"You think P.J.'s the ghost of your great-grandfather, and you think your brother's going to die in a storm today?" Jessica asked. She looked out the window at the clear blue sky.

"I *know* it sounds crazy," Sam said. "But I'm not asking you to believe me—just to help me."

"I don't think it's crazy," Elizabeth said, shaking her head. "I believe you know something about David."

"Well, if you want to stop him," Jessica suggested, "why don't you call the marina and tell them?"

"Jess, that's a great idea!" Elizabeth exclaimed, rushing for the phone book.

A minute later, Elizabeth had dialed the marina. "Hello, this is Elizabeth Wakefield," she said after a pause. "It's *extremely* important for me to get a message to Mr. Barton. He docks his boat there at the marina. He should be with his son, David." Elizabeth paused again and glanced at Sam and Jessica. "No, Wakefield. W-A-K-E-F-I-E-L-D," Elizabeth said slowly while tapping her foot impatiently. She looked exasperated. Finally she said, "Never mind who I am. Do you know who Mr. Barton is? He's with his son, David, and they're going out on a boat." She listened for a moment. "Good. You've got to stop them. I *must* speak to them. It's extremely important."

Sam's stomach tightened as he saw Elizabeth's frown.

"Please, run and stop them!" Elizabeth said urgently. "It's a matter of life and death. *Please!*"

Elizabeth looked at Sam and smiled wanly. "He said he'd go out and find them before their boat leaves the dock. Don't worry, Sam, I'm sure—what? Yes, I'm still here."

She listened for a few seconds, then put down the phone without another word. She turned back to face Sam, who was clutching Jessica's arm. Elizabeth's face was white.

"He was too late to catch them. They had already pulled away from the dock. They're headed for open water!"

Fifteen

◇

"We have to do something!" Sam cried.

"Can't we just radio a message to them and tell them to come back?" Jessica asked.

"That won't work." Sam was pacing back and forth. "I saw the boat the other day. They don't have a radio." Sam couldn't stay in the house a minute longer. He had to get to the marina, even if it was too late. He dashed outside and grabbed his bicycle.

The twins followed. "Wait!" Elizabeth called. "We'll go with you."

Jessica and Elizabeth ran for their bicycles. The three of them rode as fast and as hard as they could to the marina. It was five miles away, but Sam felt as if it was fifty. Jessica and Elizabeth had to pedal furiously to keep up with their friend.

As they were riding, the three of them looked up and saw that the sun had been obscured by black clouds. The sky was becoming menacingly dark.

"Look at the sky!" Elizabeth shouted. "I don't believe it. A storm's coming!"

Sam pedaled even faster, but soon he realized he was fighting a losing battle. The sky just kept getting darker and darker. It was the kind of raging storm that comes up very quickly and is gone just as fast. As they neared the marina, the wind blew pieces of dirt into their faces.

Sam's legs were numb from pedaling, but he didn't slow down. He was desperate to get to the marina. He had to reach David and save him somehow.

By the time they got to the marina, the sky was almost as black as night. The rain was hammering down. People on the docks were hurrying to secure their boats and find shelter.

"You kids better get inside," a woman shouted as she ran past them. "It's going to be a bad one."

Sam pushed his wet hair out of his eyes. The storm was blowing full force now, and the wind whipped the waves into white foam. Salt water splashed on both sides of the dock as the three of them ran to the end of it.

"It's all happening again!" Sam yelled over the thunder and lightning.

"I don't see them," Jessica said, using her hands to block the rain from her eyes. "Maybe they're on their way in. They'll make it, Sam. They will."

"Look!" Elizabeth shouted. She pointed out to the ocean. "There they are!"

The small motor boat looked like a toy. It bobbed up and down in the waves.

"They're yelling for help!" Sam said. "I can see them waving their arms!"

"I can't hear a thing with this wind," Elizabeth yelled.

Sam saw the boat being pushed up by the rising waves and then dropping down when the waves fell. He could see that David was gripping the sides of the boat as tightly as he could. Sam could feel his brother's fear as if it were his own.

A blast of wind suddenly blew Jessica off her feet. She slipped and fell on the dock, almost sliding over the edge and into the water. Elizabeth quickly grabbed her arm, and Sam and Elizabeth helped Jessica up. The three of them linked arms, trying to stay on their feet. They could barely see or hear each other in the rage of the storm.

The waves out in the ocean kept getting

bigger and crashing harder. Sam was holding his breath. Every time a wave rose up behind the boat, it looked as if the boat would tip over. Each time the boat righted itself.

Then an enormous black wave, like a moving wall, rose up behind the small boat and slammed down on it. The boat split apart as it turned over.

Instantly, Sam felt a chill. Even though he was aware that he was standing on the dock, he could feel everything David felt: confusion, splashing, the bitter taste of salt water. David was calling out in fear—he was drowning!

Sam felt the energy drain from his body. He couldn't breathe. An instant later he fell to the ground, unconscious.

"He's awake!" It was Elizabeth's voice. She sounded relieved.

Where am I? Sam wondered. He could hear seagulls crying, and he could see the sky, which was a very deep blue.

Elizabeth leaned over Sam. "Hi. I'm so glad you're awake. Your parents are right here."

Sam realized that he was lying on a bench, covered with blankets. He struggled to sit up. His mother hugged him and so did his father. They both looked pale and sad.

"It's going to be OK, sweetie," Mrs. Sloane said.

Then Sam saw David's mother and father. Mr. Barton was wrapped in blankets, and Mrs. Barton was holding his arm. Sam looked from one face to another. Nobody spoke.

"Where's David?" Sam asked.

Mrs. Barton leaned against her husband's shoulder and began to sob.

"A Coast Guard boat picked up David's father," Mr. Sloane told him gently. "But they haven't found David yet."

Sam couldn't stop the tears that rolled down his cheeks. The brother he had just found was lost. "I should have stopped them," he cried.

"Sam, the Coast Guard is still out there looking," David's father said in a reassuring voice. "We've got to think positively, OK?"

"If I had just figured it out faster," Sam said.

"Shh." his mother said. "There was nothing to figure out. It was just a terrible accident."

"But you don't understand, Mom. I *knew* this was going to happen!"

The adults looked at each other but didn't say anything.

"Sam really did know there was going to be a storm today," Elizabeth said.

"Sam," his mother said, "I want to take you home. You need dry clothes and some rest."

"I'm not going, Mom. I'm not going till they find David."

"I'll stay with you, Sam," Jessica said.

"Me, too," Elizabeth said firmly.

Finally Sam's parents agreed to let him stay. Sam's mother got another blanket to wrap around his shoulders, and Jessica got him a cup of hot chocolate.

Several hours went by as the Coast Guard continued its search. Everyone knew the search would have to end at sundown—at least until the following day. After waiting for what seemed like forever, Sam sat down on a wooden bench next to his father. He wanted to stay awake and watch for signs of David, but he felt exhausted. He laid his head on his father's shoulder and closed his eyes for what seemed like only a second. But when he opened them again, he found himself lying down on the bench. The blanket that had been around his shoulders was tucked in all around him, and his mother's sweater was folded up under his head. Sam felt cold all over. He knew why—he had had the nightmare again. But this time it had been different! Sam closed his eyes again, remembering.

As always, there had been the old man. He was wearing a long yellow slicker, and a wide-brimmed rain hat hid his face. He fought the wind with all of his might, leaning and pushing against it and trying to walk. Sam couldn't tell where the old man was trying to go.

Suddenly the wind blew the man's rain hat

away, and for the first time Sam saw the man's face clearly. It *was* P.J., the caretaker at the mansion!

P.J. walked on and on until he finally reached the water's edge. Then he tore off his slicker, his shoes, and his socks, and walked into the water. Deeper and deeper he went, until the water was up to his waist. Then he started swimming. The waves rose and fell, but he swam over them and under them. He slowly made his way farther and farther out to sea, into open water, far from the beach. P.J. seemed to swim forever. The sea was endless. Finally Sam saw something floating in the water. It was David! Sam couldn't tell if he was dead or alive. But P.J. swam to him, reached out, and turned him onto his back. P.J. wrapped an arm around David's chest and began to tow him through the water.

At last, P.J. pulled David onto the shore. It wasn't the beach near Sweet Valley, though. It was somewhere else, someplace Sam didn't recognize. P.J. picked David up in his arms and carried him up some stone steps toward a small wooden boathouse. Then Sam saw David sleeping, covered by a thick wool blanket.

Sam opened his eyes again. He sat up on the bench and looked around. The sky was now pink instead of blue. The sun was setting.

"Sam," his father said, walking over to the

bench and giving his son a hug, "it's getting dark. The Coast Guard says they have to stop for today. They'll look for David again tomorrow."

"Dad, I just had a dream about David. He's still alive!" Sam said. He jumped to his feet. "It's the same dream I always have. But now I finally know what it's all about. David's safe, Dad. The dream was telling me that he's OK. And I even know where he is!"

Sixteen

◇

"Dad, you've got to believe me," Sam begged his father.

Mr. Sloane was quiet for a long time. Finally he said, "Sam, we've got to go home."

Sam looked around in desperation. His mother and David's parents stood in the marina parking lot. They wouldn't believe him, either. In the other direction, the Coast Guard officers who had directed the search operation were waiting by the water's edge. They were watching their boats head back to the station after giving up the search.

Sam made a quick decision and bolted toward the water. He ran to the nearest Coast Guard officer, whose name badge said Lieutenant Liang.

"Lieutenant," Sam said quickly, "I know

where my brother is. He's alive. You've got to help me."

The lieutenant had been talking with the boats over a two-way radio. He finished his conversation and turned down the volume on his radio. Then he looked at Sam seriously. "Your name is Sam, right?"

Sam nodded.

"So's mine," said the lieutenant, shaking Sam's hand. "What did you say about your brother?"

"I *know* he's alive."

Sam's father came up and put a hand gently on Sam's shoulder. "Sam, it's time to go home now," he said. "The people here have done everything they can do for today."

"Just let me tell you, OK?" Sam said to Lieutenant Liang. His voice sounded frightened and desperate.

"Sure, Sam. Tell me," Lieutenant Liang said.

Sam described what he had seen in his dream. "It's a cabin or a boathouse. And you've got to walk up a hill from the water to get to it. There are a lot of fishing nets and stuff around the outside," he concluded.

If Lieutenant Liang believed Sam, his face didn't show it. "How did your brother get there?" he asked.

Sam took a deep breath. "Someone saved him and brought him there."

"In that storm?" Lieutenant Liang asked.

"You've got to believe me," Sam insisted. "We've got to find David. *Please*. It's an old wooden house with stone steps leading up to it."

Lieutenant Liang looked thoughtful. "Mr. Sloane," he said to Sam's father, "there *is* a log boathouse about half a mile to the south of here. And it *is* up a small hill. That's the direction the water would have pulled the boy."

"You mean you believe me?" Sam asked.

"I think it wouldn't hurt to investigate," Lieutenant Liang said. "But the boathouse is in a rocky cove, too rocky to risk taking in boats. There are no roads, either. We'd have to walk."

"No problem. I'm ready," Sam said.

Soon Elizabeth, Jessica, Sam, Lieutenant Liang, and two other Coast Guard officers were walking along the water's edge toward the boathouse. The lieutenant stayed in radio contact with Sam and David's parents.

As it grew darker, Lieutenant Liang passed out flashlights to everyone.

"Elizabeth, won't it be wonderful if we find David?" Jessica whispered to her sister.

"Yes, but I won't be surprised," Elizabeth answered. "There's something special between Sam and David."

"I know," Jessica said. "Just like us."

After they had walked for about twenty minutes, Lieutenant Liang stopped and aimed his flashlight up a small hill until the beam shone on a log building.

"That's it," Sam shouted, running up the hill. "This is the place in my dream!"

Everyone ran up the steep hill to the boat-house as fast as they could. Lieutenant Liang got to the door first. Sam was directly behind him.

Inside, the boathouse was dark and damp. Overturned rowboats crowded the small room. But there, on a handmade wooden bench, was David, covered by a thick wool blanket. Everything was exactly as Sam had dreamed it.

Suddenly David opened his eyes and raised his head. He shielded his eyes from the glare of the flashlights.

"David, it's me! It's me," Sam said, running over to his brother.

"We found him," Lieutenant Liang said into his radio. "Repeat: We found him."

A voice asked over the radio, "Is he OK?" Sam could barely make out the words over the crackle of static, but he recognized Mr. Barton's voice.

The lieutenant leaned down and put the radio near David. "Hi, Dad. I'm OK," David said in a weak voice.

Lieutenant Liang handed the radio to one of the other officers. "Can you move?" he asked David.

"I don't think I'm hurt, but I'm awfully tired," David said. Sam noticed he had several bruises on his face.

"David, how did you get here?" the lieutenant asked.

David's face clouded over. For a moment, he was silent. "When I was in the water, I was really scared," he finally said. "Then I saw Dad being picked up by the Coast Guard boat and I started yelling 'I'm over here' as loudly as I could."

"We must not have been able to hear you over the noise of the storm," Lieutenant Liang said.

"You know, it's funny," David said with a good-natured grin, "I couldn't even hear myself." He shook his head.

"What happened next?" Sam asked.

"After the boat had gone, I tried to swim for shore," David continued. "But the waves were so big that they kept pushing me under." David shivered and wrapped himself tighter in the blanket.

"But can you tell us how you got here?" Lieutenant Liang prompted him.

"I got so tired that I could hardly keep from going under. I was certain that I was going to drown. Then suddenly someone grabbed me. At first I thought it was Dad, but then I realized it couldn't be. I felt myself being pulled in some direction. I think maybe I passed out after that—I don't remember much else.''

Sam couldn't stay quiet any more. "Didn't you see him, David? Didn't you see who it was?''

"I thought I was dreaming," David said. His eyes opened wider, and he stared at his twin.

"You weren't dreaming," Sam said, shaking his head.

"What are you guys talking about?" Jessica demanded.

"When I woke up, I was here." David spoke as if he were in a trance. "I knew I was safe. A man was standing over me and smiling. It was P.J.''

"P.J.? P.J. saved your life?" Elizabeth asked.

"Yeah," David said.

"But that's impossible!" Jessica blurted out. "Why would P.J. be around? And besides, he's so old! I doubt he could swim far in that storm.''

"Look at what's under David's head, if you don't believe him," Sam said solemnly.

Someone aimed a flashlight where Sam was pointing, and in its beam they saw a plaid shirt bundled up as a pillow under David's head.

"That's P.J.'s shirt," Sam explained to the Coast Guard officers. "But David," he continued, "P.J. isn't just a caretaker. He's the ghost of our great-grandfather, Peter Burroughs.''

David nodded. "I knew it," he said. "That's why he was in our dreams.''

"I don't know anything about your dreams," Lieutenant Liang said. "But I *do* know I'd better get you back to your parents."

"That sounds great!" David agreed, with a grin.

Sam stayed at David's house that night. Even though they were exhausted, they were too excited to sleep. They got into bed because Mrs. Barton insisted, but then they lay awake and talked for hours.

"It all makes sense when you think about it," Sam said. "Thirty years ago—thirty years ago *today*!—our great-grandfather couldn't save Michael, his grandson. They both drowned. I'll bet that's why his ghost was still hanging around the old house."

"Yeah. And the dream was a message," David agreed. "He was trying to warn us about the storm."

Sam was quiet for a minute longer, still thinking about his great-grandfather's ghost. "I think he knew that even though he didn't save Michael, someday he'd be able to make up for it by saving you," Sam said.

David smiled. "I hope he feels better now."

"Do you think we'll ever see him again?" Sam asked.

"I don't know," David answered. "I hope so."

David picked up the photo of his parents in front of the Seever mansion and looked at it silently for a long time. His parents both looked so happy. Then David looked at the mansion behind them. It had once belonged to his great-grandfather—the man who had saved his life that day. But now something was different about the picture. Finally David realized what it was.

"Sam, look at this," David exclaimed.

Sam didn't see anything different until David pointed to one area of the photo—the corner upstairs window.

"Remember the face in the window?" David said. "It looked like an old man, right?"

"Right," Sam said. "Wow! It's gone! The window's empty."

Both brothers stared at the photo. Their great-grandfather's face must have been in the window. Now that he had saved David's life, he wasn't in the window any longer. He was finally at peace.

"Where'd that come from?" Sam exclaimed. "I never noticed that before!" He circled an area on the photograph with his finger. Inside the circle was what looked like the outline of a door on the side of the Seever mansion.

"I've looked at this a million times," David said. "That door was never there."

"And there's no door on that side of the house. I've been there often enough to know.

That wall's covered with ivy," Sam said with certainty. "But—maybe there's a door *under* the ivy," he added softly.

David's face brightened. "Sam, this is another message from P.J.! He's trying to tell us something—something about a door. We've got to go to the mansion tomorrow and find it!"

Jessica looked at Elizabeth and grimaced. The twins were sitting in the family room after dinner. "Do I have to?" she asked. "Couldn't you call her and tell her for me, Lizzie?"

Elizabeth shook her head. "You're the one Lila's mad at, not me."

"Oh, all right." Jessica sighed. She wished she could avoid apologizing to Lila, but she knew she had to. "Maybe if I tell Lila about what happened at the marina this afternoon, she won't mind anymore," she said hopefully.

"Maybe." Elizabeth opened her book and started reading.

Jessica stuck her tongue out at her sister, then picked up the telephone and dialed Lila's number.

"Hello?" Lila said.

"Hi," Jessica said brightly. "It's me."

"What do *you* want?" Lila muttered.

"Well, I wanted to tell you . . ." Jessica looked over at Elizabeth, who nodded firmly. "I wanted to say I'm sorry, Lila. It was a rotten trick, and I shouldn't have done it."

Lila sniffed. "It sure was a rotten trick, Jessica. Unicorns shouldn't do that kind of thing to each other."

"I know," Jessica agreed quickly. "That's why I'm really, really sorry. I'll never do anything like that again."

"Promise?"

"Promise." Jessica smiled happily at her sister. She knew Lila would forgive her! "I'll call you tomorrow, OK?" she went on.

"OK," Lila agreed. "Bye."

Jessica hung up the phone and made a V-for-victory sign in the air. "Mission accomplished!"

"She's not mad at you anymore?" Elizabeth asked in surprise.

"No way," Jessica answered proudly. "Who could stay mad at me?"

Instead of responding, Elizabeth threw a pillow at her twin. Jessica ducked and ran out of the room, laughing.

Seventeen

◇

Sam and David could hardly wait to get to the Seever mansion the next morning. Mr. Barton had made a huge pancake breakfast in honor of the twins' birthday, but they gulped down their food and soon were out the door. When they got to the mansion, the dark old house looked quiet and still. They hopped off their bikes and leaned them against the old iron fence.

"It doesn't feel as strange to me today," Sam said, hesitating outside the gate. "Before, whenever I came here I used to feel afraid. Now it's different. The house doesn't seem to be . . ." His voice trailed off.

"Haunted?" David supplied.

"Yeah. I guess that means P.J. is gone," Sam said. He was just about to slip through the open gate when a woman walked by. It was one of the next-door neighbors, the same woman Sam and the Wakefields had talked to when he had first brought the girls to the old house. The woman was walking her dog, and as she passed by she smiled at the two identical brothers.

"Hi," Sam said. Then he had an idea. "Have you seen P.J. around lately?" he asked casually.

"No, I can't honestly say that I have. Who's P.J.?" the woman asked.

"You know—the man who's the caretaker here," Sam said.

The woman looked at the Seever mansion. Sam's eyes followed hers. He saw her taking in the weed-filled yard and the peeling paint. The woman turned back to Sam and David. "A caretaker around *here*?" she said in an amused tone. She cleared her throat. "I don't think this place has ever had a caretaker." The woman's dog began tugging on its leash, and she followed it down the street. "I have to go now," she called, giving them a little wave.

"Well, that proves that we were right," David said. "P.J. wasn't the caretaker. He was our great-grandfather, Peter Burroughs—the ghost of the Seever mansion."

"Let's go," Sam said. The boys pushed open the gate and headed for the side of the house, where tangled vines of ivy grew like a second, leafy wall.

Sam started at one end and David started at the other. They worked toward the middle, feeling behind the ivy with their hands.

"It's not here," David said after a few minutes. He was clearly disappointed.

"It *is* here," Sam said. "Trust me."

"How do you know?" David asked.

"Because," Sam said with a smile, "I've got my hand on the doorknob."

Both boys started pulling at the ivy. Five minutes later they had cleared away enough ivy to reveal a small door that opened into a long-forgotten shed. The door was unlocked.

Sam took a deep breath and gave the door a push. It opened with a loud squeak. The inside of the shed was very dark. The only window was covered over by ivy. By the light from the doorway, the boys could see boxes and trunks and a few old pieces of furniture.

"What do you think is in those boxes?" David whispered.

"Let's find out," Sam said. Secretly, Sam hoped the boxes would be filled with some kind of treasure. Maybe there would be money, or chests of coins and jewels, or even a map leading them to buried treasure. But after an hour of pushing away the cobwebs and opening the dusty cartons one by one, he and David had found only old books, clothes, and magazines.

"I can't believe it," David said with a sigh. "There's nothing here but junk."

"It's not even our grandfather's junk," Sam said.

"No. It's Jeremiah Seever's. He must have never—"

"Shh!" Sam interrupted. "Listen," he hissed.

Then David heard them. Footsteps. They sounded like they were heading directly toward the secret room.

The two brothers exchanged quick looks of panic.

"Hide," Sam whispered. "Fast!" David jumped behind an old steamer trunk, and Sam scrambled under a rolltop desk.

The footsteps stopped. Then the door creaked again as someone pushed it open farther. Sam tried to swallow but his throat was too dry.

"Hi. Is anybody here?" a voice called.

"Jessica?" Sam said in surprise.

"Who's in there?"

Sam and David crawled out of their hiding places and went toward the door. It *was* Jessica, and Elizabeth was with her. Sam breathed a sigh of relief. "What are you doing here?" he demanded.

It only took a minute for Jessica to explain why she and Elizabeth had come to the house. She had lost Elizabeth's new headband the last time she had been there. She didn't tell the boys why she had been at the house that day, though.

"So we came back here to look for it," Elizabeth finished. "What are *you* guys doing in here?"

"We found a door hidden under the ivy," David said.

Jessica looked in the shed. "What are you looking for?" she asked.

David and Sam shrugged.

"Wow! Look at this old desk," Elizabeth said, suddenly noticing the old wooden rolltop tucked away in a corner. "It's beautiful."

The desk had a small tarnished brass plate on it.

"Private property of Jeremiah Seever," David read in the dim light.

"Can we look?" Jessica asked.

"The house belongs to us as much as anyone," Sam said. "Go ahead."

"I doubt you'll find anything interesting," David added.

Elizabeth carefully opened the desk. Inside she found old pens and pencils, rubber stamps, paper clips, and a rusty three-hole punch. They were about to give up finding anything interesting when Jessica pulled a large envelope tied with string from the very back of the desk's bottom drawer. Like the desk, it was marked "Personal Property of Jeremiah Seever."

"It's probably hair he saved from every hair-cut he ever had," Sam said sarcastically.

"Don't be so gross, Sam. It's just some papers," Jessica said as she pulled some folded and faded sheets from the envelope.

"Hey, look," Sam said, taking the papers from her and flipping to the last page. "These papers were signed by Jeremiah Seever and Peter Burroughs—P.J."

"It's some sort of legal document," David said as Sam examined the pages. "My parents are both lawyers. They could tell us what it's about."

"Wait!" Sam exclaimed. "P.J. said Jeremiah Seever used phony legal papers to prove that he owned this house. Do you think these papers could be the ones he used?"

"Come on," David said. "Let's go to my house." They arrived at David's house just as Mr. and Mrs. Barton were getting home from their offices.

"Where'd you get these?" Mr. Barton asked as he and his wife read the papers.

David told his parents the whole story as quickly as possible. "Are they the papers Jeremiah used to cheat P.J.?" he wanted to know.

"No, David," his mother said. "I'm afraid these aren't those phony papers. But this is the *real* agreement. These papers dissolved their business partnership. It says here that Peter Burroughs agreed to split the money from the business with Jeremiah. But there's nothing about giving away the house."

Mr. Barton smiled. "According to this, Peter agreed to pay a lot more money to Jeremiah so that the house would stay in the Burroughs family," he said.

"That must be why Jeremiah hid the papers," Elizabeth said. "They prove that the house belongs to your family, Sam."

"And not to Jeremiah Seever?" David asked Mr. and Mrs. Barton.

"Definitely not," Mrs. Barton said.

"In fact," added Mr. Barton, "I think you two are the only living relatives of the Burroughses. And if I'm right, that means the house belongs to you!"

"To us?" David said, looking at his twin brother.

Sam couldn't stop smiling. "I'll bet my dad would love to fix up that old house," he said.

The following evening a party was scheduled in honor of Sam and David's twelfth birthday. That afternoon, Jessica and Elizabeth got a phone call from David.

"The party's been moved!" he announced. "It's going to be at the Seever mansion—oops, I mean the *Burroughs* mansion!"

"You're kidding!" Elizabeth exclaimed.

"Nope," David said. "Mom and Dad went down to City Hall first thing this morning. It's not official yet, but it looks like the house is going to be half mine and half Sam's."

"Terrific!" Elizabeth exclaimed.

When Jessica and Elizabeth arrived at the Burroughs mansion for the party, they found the first floor empty and clean. Since the electricity hadn't been hooked up yet, there were dozens of tall lighted candles throughout the rooms. Elizabeth was surprised by how much more cheerful the house looked already. Jessica said it didn't feel creepy at all anymore.

But Sam and David were the biggest surprise of all. The two brothers had done something they had never done before. They wore the same shirts, the same pants, and even the same shoes. They were wearing name tags, so that nobody would get confused.

When the boys greeted Jessica and Elizabeth at the door, Jessica narrowed her eyes suspiciously. "You're wearing the wrong names!" she exclaimed.

Sam and David started to laugh. "You're the first to notice!" Sam told her.

Elizabeth laughed. "You can't fool a twin with a twin switch," she told Sam and David.

"Since you're so into being twins, you guys are going to love our presents," Jessica added.

"Matching baseball caps from the Minnesota *Twins!*"

"That's cool," Sam said, and David agreed.

A band was playing in the dining room and sixth-graders from David's school and Sweet Valley Middle School were dancing. There were two birthday cakes, a chocolate one for David and a vanilla one for Sam.

Toward the middle of the party, Jessica noticed her sister and Lila whispering together in a corner. That was strange, since Elizabeth and Lila didn't usually get along very well. But Jessica was having too much fun to think about it for long.

By eleven o'clock, everyone had gone home except for the two pairs of twins. Jessica threw herself into a chair and yawned.

"I am *so* tired," she said.

"Me, too," Elizabeth agreed. She picked up a few empty paper cups and crumpled napkins. "I'll go get another trash bag," she said, leaving the room.

Jessica stretched lazily in the big wing chair. The kind of sleepiness that came from a good party was the kind of sleepiness she liked best. She sighed happily.

"I'll be right back," Sam said. "I left my baseball cap somewhere, and I want to find it before I go home."

David snapped his fingers. "That reminds me," he said to no one in particular. He left the room through another door.

Jessica looked around and smiled in satisfaction. The party had been the perfect way to end spring vacation. Of course, going back to school was something she didn't want to have to think about. She would rather just think back over what a great vacation it had been.

The one thing she would always remember, she decided, was how many eerie things had happened. Now that it was all over it was funny to think how scared she had been of the Burroughs mansion. It was really just a big, empty old house. There was nothing particularly scary about that. But she still shivered remembering how spooked she had been.

She looked around again and suddenly felt a tiny tingle of nervousness. Where was everybody?

"Elizabeth?" she called out. She stood up. "David? Sam?" she called a little louder.

Nothing but silence answered her.

Jessica swallowed hard. Then she laughed. "OK, you guys. Very funny. Come on, let's go home, Lizzie. I'm exhausted."

The drafty old mansion was still and silent. *Just like a tomb*, Jessica thought.

"Fine, have it your way," Jessica muttered.

"You can't scare me. I can wait as long as you can."

She walked around the room, humming under her breath. Every few seconds she darted a quick look into one corner or another. Then she tiptoed to the door, slowly turned the knob, and yanked it open.

"Aha!" she yelled, sure they were waiting there to jump out at her.

But the hallway beyond was empty and dark.

Jessica shut the door carefully and bit her lip. She was beginning to get worried.

But that's just what they're hoping for, she realized. Jessica was determined not to let them think she was frightened.

"It doesn't bother me," she called out in a cheerful voice. "I can wait here all night, you guys! You might as well give up now!" She rocked back and forth on her heels. "But this *is* getting boring, you know!"

Suddenly there was a soft tap on the floor behind her. She spun around and saw a paper cup roll away under the table. Another paper cup rolled to the edge of the table and fell off with a ping. Jessica let out her breath.

"There must be a draft," she said aloud to reassure herself. She paced back and forth a few more times, snapping her fingers. When she couldn't stand to wait any longer, she grabbed a flashlight off a table, strode to the door and went out into the hallway. She almost wished the others would jump out and scare her and get their joke over with. She walked down the hall, peering into each room on the first floor. The flashlight beam was like a long, bright sword probing into the dark. It made Jessica feel a little bit braver.

At last she realized that she was the only person on the first floor. Jessica squared her shoulders and climbed the stairs. "Come on out, you guys," she called. "Jump out and scream at me, will you? I'm getting pretty fed up with this game. It's not funny anymore!"

Jessica searched the second floor rooms one by one, but they were empty, too. At least she *thought* they were. She certainly wasn't going to look under the beds or into the closets.

As she paused in the upstairs hallway, she heard a soft thump on the ceiling.

"Finally," she sighed. "Now I know where you all are."

She started up the narrow stairs to the third floor, and her heart began to hammer away like a drum. The stairs creaked under her feet. She reached the third floor and waved the flashlight back and forth. There were cobwebs everywhere, and lots of dust. One door with a thin sliver of light showing at the bottom stood at the end of the hallway.

"OK," she said under her breath. "This is

it." She walked slowly down the hallway. She couldn't guess what was behind the door—probably something horrible and scary. There was only one way to find out.

She reached one trembling hand out to the doorknob, twisted it, and pushed the door open.

Her flashlight shone on Elizabeth, David, and Sam, sitting on the floor. There was one candle in the middle of their circle. It shed a soft glow on the room.

"Hi, Jess," Elizabeth said in an apologetic voice, looking up. "We were just sitting here talking. I guess we forgot you were waiting."

"Right, we just got into this conversation," Sam explained with a sheepish smile.

Jessica stared at them. She shook her head in disbelief. "Are you kidding me?" she gasped. "I've been frightened half to death!"

"Sorry." David said. "We should have called you."

"This is unbelievable," Jessica muttered. "I was positive you guys were trying to scare the life out of me."

Then she noticed that Elizabeth was gazing at something past her. Elizabeth's eyes widened in fear.

Jessica whirled around.

"Wroooaaaa!" roared a dark figure in the hallway behind her.

Jessica screamed at the top of her lungs and covered her face with her hands.

"I got you, Jessica!" Lila said, bursting into laughter.

"Wow," Jessica said weakly. She drew a deep breath and looked at the others. "You guys really had this planned, didn't you? You pretended to leave and then snuck back in, right, Lila?"

Sam and David began to laugh.

"I'm sorry, Jess," Elizabeth said. She jumped up and gave her twin a big hug. "I didn't think you'd be so scared."

Lila smiled. "It was a pretty good scare, wasn't it?"

"It sure was," Jessica agreed. She looked at Lila, and had to grin. "I guess we're even now, right?"

"I guess we are," Lila said.

"OK," Jessica said. She looked at the others. "*Now* can we go home?"

"Absolutely," Elizabeth said. She smiled at the two guys. "Thanks for a great party."

"Best party of the vacation," Lila added.

Jessica shook her finger in her friend's face. "If you ever pull a stunt like that again . . ."

"I will," Lila warned, "if *you* ever pull a stunt like that again."

Jessica laughed.

* * *

"I can't believe school starts Monday," Elizabeth remarked as she and Jessica were getting ready for bed that night.

"Monday? Oh, Lizzie, I forgot to tell you. You know how this is our last No-Cooking Monday coming up? Well, I promised Lila I'd help her decide how to get her hair cut that day. And since I really have to be nice to her now, I might not get home in time to help you. But don't worry, Elizabeth, I'll definitely be here to eat with you. Dad said I couldn't miss another Monday night dinner."

"No problem, Jess," Elizabeth said in a cheery voice.

"You're not mad at me?" Jessica demanded. She was clearly surprised—and suspicious.

"Jess, really, I don't mind at all. I want to cook dinner by myself, honest." Elizabeth's smile broadened.

"Why don't I believe you?" Jessica asked uncertainly.

Elizabeth widened her eyes and held out her hands. "Believe me! Believe me!"

Jessica slowly went to the door, frowning. "OK," she said, sounding very reluctant.

"But you could help, if you want," Elizabeth added. She gave Jessica an angelic smile. "Not that I'm asking you to, you know."

At the door, Jessica stopped and turned around. She looked at Elizabeth through narrowed eyes for a moment. "You're planning something, aren't you?" she said after a long pause.

"What are you talking about? I'm planning dinner, if that's what you mean," Elizabeth replied. She picked up her hairbrush and began to brush her hair.

"Yeah, but you've got a funny look in your eyes," Jessica said as she came back to stand in front of Elizabeth.

Elizabeth pretended to be surprised. "What look?" she asked.

"*That* look. *My* look," Jessica said. She stared hard at Elizabeth. "Are you planning to do something to get me back for making you do all of the other No-Cooking Mondays?" she demanded.

"Jessica, why would I do that?" Elizabeth said, trying not to smile. "Especially after that joke we played on you at the party. You're probably just still feeling suspicious because of that."

"Well, who could blame me?" Jessica said.

"Nobody," Elizabeth said. "But you've got the wrong idea. I'm very happy to cook dinner by myself. I *want* to do it," she insisted. She smiled sweetly at her sister.

"Oh no you don't," Jessica said. She shook her head emphatically. "You're trying to fool me, Elizabeth Wakefield. It won't work. *I'm* cooking dinner that night, so you can just forget about whatever little scheme you were thinking up."

Elizabeth shrugged and got under her covers. "I don't know what you're talking about, but if that's the way you feel about it . . ."

"It is," Jessica said. "So don't even go near the kitchen on Monday night or you'll regret it."

"I won't," Elizabeth said, crossing her heart and snapping her fingers. "I promise."

By five-thirty on Monday, Jessica was frantic. When she had tried to shake the water off the vegetables, they had fallen out of the colander and onto the floor. The macaroni had stuck together in one big gummy mess, and the sauce was burned.

Jessica had assumed that making tuna casserole and salad would be a snap. But the only thing that was snapping so far was her patience. As she crossed the kitchen floor, she squashed a piece of tomato under her heel.

"Oh, yuck!" she groaned.

"What's for dinner?" Steven asked, poking his head in the doorway.

Jessica glared at him. "Get out of here!" she ordered, cleaning up the tomato with a paper towel.

"Sorr—eee," he said, ducking out of sight. "By the way," he added, looking in again, "did you know you have some kind of brown goop on your face?"

"Out!" Jessica said. She grabbed a dish towel and wiped her face with it. Then she stared at the disaster she had made of dinner and took a deep breath. There had to be a simple way out of it.

"I can just wash these off again," she decided, looking at the vegetables. She glared at the solid mass of macaroni and made a face. Then she dumped it into the garbage can.

"How's dinner coming along?" Mr. Wakefield asked, stepping in through the patio door.

Jessica turned to give him an anguished look. "It's not ready yet, Dad," she said.

"OK. Just asking." He hurried out.

For a moment, Jessica shut her eyes. What a mess! It was a good thing dessert was easy. She decided to check on the jello. Jello was impossible to wreck.

Feeling a little more hopeful, Jessica opened the refrigerator and pulled out the long dish of orange gelatin with banana slices. But it began sloshing and slipping around as she moved the dish. It was still liquid, even after an hour in the refrigerator.

"What?" Jessica gasped. "What did I do wrong *this* time?" She stared at the orange and banana soup and shook her head. Then she noticed a package of American cheese slices on the top shelf of the refrigerator.

Gritting her teeth, Jessica grabbed the cheese, a jar of mayonnaise, and some leftover lettuce and began to make cheese sandwiches. They had to eat *something* for dinner, after all.

"How's it coming?" Mrs. Wakefield asked, stepping into the kitchen.

Jessica stood with her back to the sandwiches. "Fine, Mom. Nothing to worry about."

"Are you making something special?" her mother asked with a smile.

"Well, I guess you could say that," Jessica agreed uncertainly. "But I need privacy for this creation, Mom. I hope you don't mind."

"Of course not, sweetie. I'm so glad I don't have to cook, I'd even eat a sandwich." Mrs. Wakefield laughed cheerfully.

Jessica forced herself to smile until her mother left the room. Then she turned around and scowled at the cheese sandwiches. They looked awfully plain. Maybe if she dressed them up a little bit . . .

For the next several minutes she worked feverishly. She cut all the sandwiches in triangles and placed a sprig of parsley on each piece, put two kinds of pickles on each plate, rewashed the vegetables and tossed them in a bowl with some salad dressing. Then she quickly set the table, turned the lights off, and lit some candles.

"OK," she called out. She crossed her fingers.

The rest of her family trooped into the dining room and sat at their places. Mr. Wakefield had a big smile on his face. "Well, it looks very romantic in here. Let's see what—" He broke off when he saw what dinner was.

Nobody spoke for a long moment.

"Cheese sandwiches?" Steven asked in disbelief. "I hope there's something good for dessert."

Jessica smiled wanly.

Elizabeth picked up a piece of parsley and nibbled on it. "Looks good to me," she said. "In fact, I think this is the best No-Cooking Monday yet." She looked at her sister and grinned. "Thanks for cooking, Jessica."

"You're welcome," Jessica said. She glanced at her twin suspiciously. If she didn't know better, she would have thought Elizabeth had planned it that way.

But that would just be letting her imagination run away with her again, wouldn't it?

We hope you enjoyed reading this book. If you would like to receive further information about available titles in the Bantam series, just write to the address below, with your name and address: Kim Prior, Bantam Books, 61–63 Uxbridge Road, Ealing, London W5 5SA.

If you live in Australia or New Zealand and would like more information about the series, please write to:

Sally Porter
Transworld Publishers
(Australia) Pty Ltd
15–23 Helles Avenue
Moorebank
NSW 2170
AUSTRALIA

Kiri Martin
Transworld Publishers (NZ) Ltd
3 William Pickering Drive
Albany
Auckland
NEW ZEALAND

All Bantam and Young Adult books are available at your bookshop or newsagent, or can be ordered from the following address: Corgi/Bantam Books, Cash Sales Department, PO Box 11, Falmouth, Cornwall, TR10 9EN.

Please list the title(s) you would like, and send together with a cheque or postal order to cover the cost of the book(s) plus postage and packing charges of £1.00 for one book, £1.50 for two books, and an additional 30p for each subsequent book ordered to a maximum of £3.00 for seven or more books.

(The above applies only to readers in the UK, and BFPO)

Overseas customers (including Eire), please allow £2.00 for postage and packing for the first book, an additional £1.00 for a second book, and 50p for each subsequent title ordered.

Created by Francine Pascal

Jessica and Elizabeth Wakefield have had lots of adventures in *Sweet Valley High* and *Sweet Valley Twins* . . .

Now read about the twins at age seven! All the fun that comes with being seven is part of *Sweet Valley Kids*. Read them all!

1. SURPRISE! SURPRISE!
2. RUNAWAY HAMSTER
3. THE TWINS' MYSTERY TEACHER
4. ELIZABETH'S VALENTINE
5. JESSICA'S CAT TRICK
6. LILA'S SECRET
7. JESSICA'S BIG MISTAKE
8. JESSICA'S ZOO ADVENTURE
9. ELIZABETH'S SUPER-SELLING LEMONADE
10. THE TWINS AND THE WILD WEST
11. CRYBABY LOIS
12. SWEET VALLEY TRICK OR TREAT
13. STARRING WINSTON EGBERT
14. JESSICA THE BABYSITTER
15. FEARLESS ELIZABETH
16. JESSICA THE TV STAR
17. CAROLINE'S MYSTERY DOLLS
18. BOSSY STEVEN
19. JESSICA AND THE JUMBO FISH
20. THE TWINS GO INTO HOSPITAL

SUPER SNOOPER EDITIONS

1. THE CASE OF THE SECRET SANTA

THE SADDLE CLUB

Bonnie Bryant

Share the thrills and spills of three girls drawn together by their special love of horses in this adventurous series.

1. HORSE CRAZY
2. HORSE SHY
3. HORSE SENSE
4. HORSE POWER
5. TRAIL MATES
6. DUDE RANCH
7. HORSE PLAY
8. HORSE SHOW
9. HOOF BEAT
10. RIDING CAMP
11. HORSE WISE
12. RODEO RIDER
13. STARLIGHT CHRISTMAS
14. SEA HORSE
15. TEAM PLAY
16. HORSE GAMES
17. HORSENAPPED
18. PACK TRIP
19. STAR RIDER
20. SNOW RIDE
21. RACE HORSE
22. FOX HUNT

Forthcoming:

23. HORSE TROUBLE
24. GHOST RIDER